KU-167-932

'Narrated with spectacular economy, in a thudding, rhythmic staccato studded with local vernacular, the book deftly folds themes of pride, masculinity and ecological ruin into its central story: the visceral vengeance quest that ensues after a fellow miner makes off with Michael's life-changing haul of gold'

***Observer* Best Debut Novelists of 2022**

'Here we see the Industrial Revolution (and by extension, the British empire) as it really was: merciless and driven entirely by greed and exploitation. Wiles's writing throughout is as chiselled and pure as the sedimentary rock from which carbonised coal is created … *Mercia's Take* is a powerful tribute to all those who toiled at the coalfaces across Britain so that an avaricious empire might expand, whatever the cost'

Guardian

'With his mastery of Black Country dialect and rugged prose stripped to the bone, the author has produced a brilliantly evocative novel of the time when men were in harness to the harsh and unforgiving landscape of Mercia (the ancient name for the region)'

Daily Mail

'This debut marks Wiles as a formidable talent'

The Times

'A story of Old Testament force and simplicity'

TLS

'Daniel Wiles channels the Southern Gothic into the vernacular of the Black Country and unearths from the past a tale of desperation that speaks to our current damnation. A striking debut'

Paul Lynch

'A powerful, wrought fable. The story, and the prose itself, seem driven by sheer will. And that resounds long after the pages of the book fall closed'

Cynan Jones

Daniel Wiles

Mercia's Take

SWIFT PRESS

This paperback edition published by Swift Press 2022
First published in Great Britain by Swift Press 2022

1 3 5 7 9 10 8 6 4 2

Copyright © Daniel Wiles 2022

The right of Daniel Wiles to be identified as the Author of this Work has been asserted in accordance with the Copyright, Designs and Patents Act 1988.

Typeset by Tetragon, London
Printed and bound in Great Britain by CPI Group (UK) Ltd, Croydon, CRO 4YY

A CIP catalogue record for this book is available from the British Library

ISBN: 9781800750845
eISBN: 9781800750708

Mercia's Take

I

MICHAEL stood in the cage. It was about ten feet wide and long. A dozen other men followed. Squeezed tight. Michael wore an ashen grey cotton shirt that had once been white. Outside the cage men and women moved around the vast sea of black land, down its hills and banks, in and out of its offices. He watched them. Women unhooked and hauled tubs of coal from the pithead and sent them down the bank. The giant pit wheel breathed slow and incessant. He stood as each other man, soldierlike with caged eyes. Waiting.

Winter soon.

He looked down at the man who spoke. A fellow hewer. Already halfnaked and bearing scars across his chest that scored his sootfogged skin. His stature unusually small. His hands unusually large. Michael recognised him.

Suppose weem paired up.

Ow's that? the fellow hewer said.

Lawrence day tell ye?

Work me stall. Cor spake to that cunt.

Needn't bite hands that feed ye.

Juss doe fancy spakin to him is all.

Westward groups of gulls laughed. Central to the bank the giant chimney sicked up stormblack smoke, creating a lingering baldachin. The steam engines rattled loud and hot, a constant alarm. Dead leaves from surrounding woodland carried across the ground by autumnal wind. Magpies and crows amongst the black earth. How many of the former were good fortune?

So, what was ye told? the fellow hewer said, looking up to him and smiling with his last few teeth different shades of brown.

That om to be paired up wi someone who looks as ye. Cain, is it?

Ar.

Michael.

So yowm new.

Ar.

Where frum?

Brownhills, Michael said, turning to Cain, who still stared at him with that partial smile plugged with chewing tobacco. His face viewed better now. Around the mouth a scratched patchy beard dyed with soot and slick with oil. His nose daftly small like a shirt pocket button and stabbing silver eyes that shone oddly bright.

The huge iron chain that held the cage started to move. Mechanical breaks like the cracking of fingerbones. The cage sunk and with it the miners. Everyone started to undress to their long johns and held their clothes clutched against their groins. Dark grey light swapped for the hot glow of Davy lamps and candles. The heat bathed them slowly from toe to head.

Chokedamp, sweat and manure invaded Michael's nostrils. The shouts of the colliers and snap of the hewers picking at the walls. As the cage was swallowed into the belly of the earth he looked up and saw a child peering over the lip of the mine.

This earth takes its workers from an early age. Never got used to the sight. How could he. It was supposed to be outlawed now, supposed to be getting better. But it seemed each time he stepped onto this working land, it was one child more. One child more and eventually we can forget it was outlawed in the first place.

The cage hit the floor. Everyone stepped off. The workers replaced by the morning shift oozed lazily from the sump and onto the cage. The cheerful noise they brought with them that could only be described as end of shift excitement, left with them up the shaft. The wind gone now. Air stagnant and damp. Michael looked about him whilst the other men spoke to the underground manager.

Ours is five, Cain shouted.

They left their clothes in buckets on the sump floor and picked up Davy lamps and walked down the inbye. Immediately they were met by a young boy with iron chains around his waist. He was pulling a small skip of coal along the narrow track road. The boy was covered in erosions where the chains rubbed against his skin. He looked up at the men. They moved. He carried on.

Michael looked down at him again and noticed twinkling blisters all about his body that were bleeding from the centre. The boy winced with each step. The only part of his face left free of black were the lines around his eyes. He fell to his knees and slowly took off his chains. Their links clanged against each other before dropping to the floor with a dull thud. He approached the undermanager, who presently took a stick that he kept under his wing and started whipping him.

Leave the nipper, Michael said.

The undermanager looked at him from up the inbye, inclined so he had three feet on him. Cain nudged Michael and said, Less goo.

Through the crowd of miners, the undermanager's dark shape was fixed on him.

The central pit was a fair size, and on the far side there were channels that led to different stalls. The ground was logged with deep black water that held glowing shapes reflected from the lamplight. Moving and dancing. Wooden beams supporting the ceiling disappeared into the water. Men waded through it ignorant of its murk and scum that varnished the surface. Cain and Michael did also.

They walked past the unsteady fire of a furnace that moved foul gases and smells of the mine haphazardly through an upcast.

Two boys emerged from a small air hole. They looked unhuman, like some blind, bald rodents unearthing themselves in search of scraps of candlelight.

This he had saw before, it was he fifteen years ago. Picked up by a man after midnight and worked until sundown. He saw the darkness. He saw the nothing. In the winter, he would go months without feeling the sun on his face. But kids always preferred this job to haulage work. It was frightening and dangerous, but without the pain of iron chains pulling on the skin, the odd shapes that spectred yellow on the wall. The angry men. The ache. The tire. The fear of the undermanager's whip.

He reached into his trouser pocket and lit a candle with his lamp and handed it to the boy. When the child took it he realised it was a girl. She handled it like a timid squirrel taking a nut. The two children, stark naked, held the candle carefully between them. It was as if they were praying to it. It lit up their faces blotted with soot. Already it dripped onto their hands and ran down their wrists. They burrowed back into the vein of the mine. He moved into the arteries.

From there the mine took three different directions. Each artery had only enough room for men to crouch-walk. Michael was a tall man and struggled to fit in them at all. The sweating body scratched by the rough walls. Cain moved down the tunnel with ease. Inside these walls clews of grey worms earthlodged.

At each stall the mine opened up a bit where the miners were already at work with pickaxes. The clap of sharp shots. He shouted at them when they swung back and almost hit him. One man on stall three turned and stared at him. He was bald, looked around fifty and had burn scars covering most of his face. Monstrous and devoid of all facial expressions.

When he reached the fifth stall Cain was already busy on it. It was hardly opened up at all. Indented about four feet tunnelside. He placed his Davy lamp on the floor and knelt and took off his boot and shook the water from it and after doing the same with the other he lifted the pickaxe and struck it against the coal. Then the two of them spoke in between pops of pickaxe.

Why do that? Cain said.

What.

The lad.

Any a nipper.

Doe trouble yaself wi it.

Ye got young a yown?

No response. Michael stole a look to his side as they hit the surface at a steady pace.

Boy has a choice to work the mine, Cain said.

Doe know that.

Is yown workin down ere?

Ay of age yet. Doe want him down ere though. Thass why om workin two mines now, so he can goo to school.

Ow old bin he?

Six.

So yowm still workin up Brownhills?

Ar.

Hewin?

On aulage mostly.

Cain stopped. The blood orange marble from the Davy lamp lit up his wide black eyes. Well I doe know if yowm more sense than stupid, he said.

A few hours into the shift. Empty tubs were pushed along the tunnel track to each stall. The miners loaded only decent sized pieces of coal into them. The breakaway pieces, or slack, were small, thin and slatelike. They were raked and saved for their own tub at end of shift.

When their tub was loaded with good coal it was pulled down the track by one of the boys. Michael watched the chains tighten around the lad and shook his head. Cain day stop hewing the wall.

Everything moved in the mine like finetuned machinery. The song of the hewers met with the melodies of the haulers and hellish bellowing of the undermanager. Every now and then they stopped for breaks, and if they could afford it, had their snap.

The snap was usually in the form of a sandwich. They used timber to sit on and the coalface to rest against. It was the same wall that they earned their money from, that they pissed against, that they cursed for shooting off bits of soot and dust that clawed at their throats and sent them into mean fits of coughing.

The coughing was a symptom of the job. Once the black gets in, it woe leave. It can only get worse. Only thing you can do is keep it at arm's length.

Michael spoke not a word more to Cain. They sat quietly for five minutes, chewing their bits of bread. Sniffing. Coughing. Scratching their heads.

◆

His shift ended. He and the other men and women were loaded back onto the cage and spewed from the mine. First stop was the checkweighman's office.

The wooden beams held up a small shack that wor built for comfort. The checkweighman was sat at a desk under a lamp with his books. He was weighing the last few tubs as the last of the feeble day lingered in the room.

The men lined up for their payslips. When the miners at stall five got theirs, Cain snarled at the checkweighman.

The fuck is this?

Under the glow of the lamplight the checkweighman was hunched over his desk. He turned his eye to Cain and at the same time pulled his shoulder up and hunched over even more. Not this again, he said.

We sent five full tubs out today.

I juss weigh em an write it down. Forget yow elected me for this job?

Cain laughed. I day elect ye for nothin.

Next, the checkweighman said.

Michael folded the slip into his pocket and walked around the shack and watched the light fall away from the sky.

Michael in the payroll office. As each one left the room another was asked, Scrip or bob? And when he reached the front he was asked the same.

He already was paid in scrip tokens for the tommy shop at his first work. Easier that way. The mine always stocked the tommy well, and it was right next door. The tommy shop here was the same. But he asked for a few bob instead. He had it worked out. His first work was for scrip, and this one for bob. He wanted to visit Pelsall village with it and a sense of achievement in his pocket.

The man took his payslip. Bob's less value than tokens, ye know that? he said, looking up at Michael over his spectacles.

Michael frowned. Why?

Juss the way it is. If ye want cash then we take away a percentage.

He arrived just before closing. A family should never look upon a loaf a bread as luxury, the baker said, shuffling about behind the counter. Keep this un, pay me next time.

Can pay for it, Michael said, handing across the coin.

The village empty save a few partied crows and pigeons in dead trees that lined the streets and rowdy dregs that hung outside the pub. A shout of accusation. Jeering of a crowd. Towards the south a red glowing skyline. The sun long set. This crude painting the living beast of industry, the chosen child to the earth's breast with its perfect heart beating metronomically throughout the night. He held the loaf under his arm and walked.

Along the cut desolation of light save the distant glow of the fires and furnaces. He trudged through mucked puddles, each of his boots sticking for a second before being sucked back out. Nesting coots squeaked from the reeds on the opposite bank. Nocturnal mallards huddled with beaded eyes watching him pass. Clouds of gnats about his head. Swifts swung about screaming from hedgerow to hedgerow.

Fork lightning over the horizon. Whitish purple against the red. A figure came. He day notice it until it was five feet ahead. It was a lad. He was bleeding down his neck and his cream shirt was ripped loose at the arm. Deep gurgling thunder. The lad went past him, head down but looking up at Michael from the corners of his eyes. Turbulent quacks of ducks. He turned around. The lad was sprinting barefoot down the cut.

He walked to the new iron bridge. Used it to cross the cut and followed a path until he arrived at a small bungalow. From outside a small haven from the smoke and rain. Warm yellow windowlight. He wiped his boots on the brown bristled mat, opened the door, and walked in.

II

He leaned on the doorframe to slip off his boots. The smell of hot gravied soup. A voice shouted from the kitchen.

What? he said.

Juss in time, she said, drying her hands with a darkened tea towel. He handed the bread to his wife of five years, Jane. Her hands were small but aged, with large knuckles and rough skin. She wore an offwhite apron over a long grey dress. It reached the floor and masked her figure. She had mousey blonde hair tied back tightly save for a few thin strands that fell down the sides of her rosy cheeks. Her eyes were small and black. Thank yow, she said, washin before tea?

Ar, he said.

He removed his clothes and followed her to the back

door. She swung it open and handed him a metal bucket. The rain had started to beat down harder. He took the bucket along the small brick path that led to the well. He yanked the pump a handful of times and waited. The smack of the water from the tap almost drowned out by the rain.

Inside the outhouse, he knelt and plunged his black hands into the water and lifted it up over his head and face and down the back of his neck. When he heard a tapping noise, he rubbed his eyes clear and turned to it. Luke was standing there holding a light.

Alright son, he said, and continued to scrub himself.

Ready for tea?

In a minute.

He sat himself down next to Jane as she spooned the stew into bowls. His face clean.

The boy started on his stew too quickly. He spat it back out and held his hand to his mouth.

Now look what yowve done. Remember to blow on it, Jane said.

Michael grabbed some bread and forced it in and around the bowl and soggied it. He looked at Jane, slowly blowing on her spoonful before tentatively eating. She was smiling. He rarely saw her without one. She caught him staring. He shifted his eyes towards Luke.

School soon, he said, to which the boy nodded and carried on blowing on his spoon. Doe let em bully ye. Yowm startin late but iss better than never. Enjoy it.

The coal fire burned with a rumble and spat every now and then. He cor tell whether the boy was excited or not. It was possible he felt neither excitement nor worry.

After the boy was put to bed, Michael sat with Jane as she sewed the holes in his socks. She was perched on the chair next to the fire. He lay on his back supported by his elbow and warmed his eyes by the fire.

Ow was the new place then? she said.

Alright. Met a strange bloke. Name was Cain.

Oh ar?

Ar. I reckon him a fruitcake.

Why?

Juss the way he carried himself. Queer way about him.

Always so quick to judge people, Michael.

He thought me mad for tekkin up two jobs.

I think yow mad for it an all.

Om alright, he said, closing the hot lids of his eyes to rest the lenses from the heat.

She stopped sewing. I wish I could help, she said. I feel like a bother.

He shook his head and looked down at his fingers. Cleared the dirt from his nails on his left hand with the corner of his righthand thumbnail. Nay. Nay. Yowm not.

The fire sank into every part of him, wrapping around him like a coat. If only it had been him and not her that them skips fell on. If only. Laid up in bed for months and changed forever. If she were in his boots, she would understand why he day find her a bother, why they could nay help their lot and he day blame her for it. Still, they never spoke of the accident in depth. What repercussions it caused. How it changed her. It happened before they met after all, and he day want to prod too much. Over the years he had thought about mentioning it in passing, in a lighthearted way, as though they were talking about the weather. What did it feel like when they came down on ye? When did ye find out ye was barren? What did that feel like then? But the words would never form. How do ye ask someone of such things?

III

It was almost ten at night when he left home. He had to walk along the cut for a mile before he reached the Brownhills colliery. Again he walked the sludgy canalside where bats fluttered about the old trees.

Ossdrawn barges churned up silt from the cut floor as they slithered past. Barges hauling coal, barges hauling limestone, barges that held families and pilgrims. One boat held so many people that some nippers even swam behind it in the dark water, only visible by the light that hung behind the boat. Dogs swam with them, their eyes reflecting like buoyed beacons.

As he got closer to the colliery he saw the lights and heard the noise. Engines and waggons and people. Heat drew upon him like a daemonic wind. Geese westward against the pale waning moon.

He crossed the far side of the bank. Past the pit wheels and the bankswomen. Past two young girls clinging to their mother's feet, sobbing painful words.

There wor a cage that he entered in this mine. Instead he stepped down a narrow turnpike staircase. He walked along the wide, hewed hallways filled with osses dragging carts as men whipped them. Lights filled the walls.

He navigated the mine easily, travelling from tunnel to crosscut to tunnel to crosscut until he reached the main pit and reported to the undermanager.

Michael, ow bist?

Fit as a fiddle, and ye?

Back's bin killin me.

Yowm walkin ay ya?

Ar?

So yowm fit. Ought to see some a these nippers.

The undermanager drew back, inverted his chin and looked at him sourly. Anyroad, he said, we ay got work on haulin for ye tonight. This is comin from above. Few a the osses keeled over, so.

Well I can work without em. Tay a problem.

We ay got enough men to push ya waggon. Them waggons am too big. Ye cor do it alone.

I car believe theym up for losin ow much money on a wasted waggon tonight?

I told ye, iss from above. Them Morris girls ay well so ye can work trappin.

Trappin?

Ar, he said, taking a pencil from behind his ear and turning his attention to his clipboard. Ye can trap or come back in the morra. Your choice.

The darkness swallowed everything. He had been sat there for hours opening and closing the trapdoor, forcing the foul gases out the mine.

He had taken the job of a child. The job of his childhood. All about the mine the sounds were various, but in this small corridor it was silent. The only noise was that of the sighing and whistling air that sought to escape around the door.

Memories form like pictures, but these memories were absent of any, for pictures need light and a child working and living in perpetual dark therefore yielded only dark. These memories were born out of fear. The feeling of it. The shaking. The crying. The whinging for his mother. The spectral hum of escaping draught.

And the true memories, those made up of pictures, were almost all of his father, and aside from the spare fishing trip down the lake, they were all fearful an all. Fear of the beatings, fear of the work. His father punching through glass windows. His mother lying against the pigsty that held no pigs. The feral dogs slinking by the cut and watching him standing with a broken arm.

And he remembered thinking, if people could see inside the house or into the garden then why cor He. If He looked then he would know what it was like.

And now that man, his father, aged as leather, sits idle and mad not knowing anything save the mines and random useless things like when he used to keep those bloody racing pigeons.

It had been a while. The old man could even be dead. If a man is destined to be his son's grandfather, then the son needed to be different. This he knew.

He was thumped awake on his temple. He winced and jumped to his feet and there stood two men each holding a Davy lamp. The light was strangling his eyes. He held his hand up to his face and squinted through his fingers. The one who had hit him was a large balding man. The other was the undermanager.

They took him topside and into a small brick building with a thatched roof that was on the east side of the colliery bank. He asked them what was going on but they said nothing.

Inside: a kidneyshaped desk next to a fireplace with

small wooden chairs either side. A bureau with papers stacked in the corner. He was sat on the chair that faced the wall. The undermanager nodded to the balding man and said, Ye can goo now.

He left and held the door open for a tall man that had to duck his head to enter the office. Michael had never seen him before. He wore a black suit with black shirt and tie and black hat. He rested his palm on the shoulder of the undermanager and whispered in his ear before sitting down opposite Michael.

The undermanager left.

The tall man removed his hat and ran his long white fingers through his blonde hair. He had clouded white eyes swallowed by his pale skin. When he spoke, he angled his gaze slightly above Michael.

You fell asleep, he said.

Michael looked down and frowned as if he saw some strange creature that showed its existence to him for the first time.

You see, our mine is like a timepiece. If any of the parts stop working, the whole thing unravels. If a trapper falls asleep and neglects to control the airflow, gases build up—

Know ow it works.

So you understand the importance. I assumed that someone who falls to sleep by the trapdoor must not know.

I apologise. Was meant to be on aulage.

An apology followed by an excuse is quite something.

If I had bin on aulage as om meant to be, I woe a fell asleep is all.

You started work in Pelsall Hall colliery today, did you not.

Ar. Michael squinted at the man, whose eyes were still searching vaguely across the room.

The man instantly pushed back his chair and walked to the door and opened it and held his hand outward and said, Please leave and do not come back.

IV

HE watched the fire. The faint halo of thin flame over ashen coals. He was unwashed and sunk low in the chair with his chin resting on his chest. His eyes were glazed over with liquid fireglow. The distant bark of a fox outside.

Footsteps.

Time is it? Jane said.

He day answer her and continued to stare into the fire. She walked over and prodded him.

What?

Yowm back early.

Was sacked.

She stood silently for a while. He still day take his eyes from the flames. The bark of the fox was louder. Shrill, rhythmic.

She finally spoke. Sacked? Juss so?

Ar.

Why?

They ave it in for me since they know about me second work.

Is that what they said? Why, they cor juss do such a thing.

He watched a spent grey coal crumble and fall from the hearth. Well, they did, he said.

Come to bed. There's still Pelsall. Thank heavens there's still Pelsall. Imagine if yow day get that job.

He finally turned to her. She was stood in her cheap nightclothes holding a candlestick. He exhaled. Then od still ave me fust job.

He rose from bed a few hours later. Looked down at his wife. The unfamiliar shape she made in the bed. She was right. At least he had work. But now he had to start again. He needed more. Luke was fast asleep. Michael left a kiss on his head and left.

The dawn was smoking and a thick mist dragged along the canal. Around halfway, he left the cut and headed westward.

Michael across the fields filled with barley and rye. A sea of golden yellow that harboured flying insects and made a great rasping as the wind licked them. The steel flash of the sun stabbed through cloud and created a pleasant morning not often seen in this country. He wor used to walking this way in the morning where the birds in the hedgerows tweeted excitedly, fluttering and dancing from branch to branch gaily, and he day rush or stumble but stopped every now and then to observe them, to observe the sky in its bright wonderful haze. He followed the track that led to the Mercia trail and stepped down from a bridge onto the cut again.

The approach of heavy smoke. White birds beckoning. He walked.

At the colliery he went to the small brick building with parked osses outside. He knocked on the door.

Come in.

He walked in and wiped his boots on the mat. Shut the door behind him. Sorry, can I ave a word, Lawrence?

Sitting across a desk was the colliery manager. He had bright red hair and regularly looked as if he was waiting in a long queue. Course, Lawrence said.

Michael sat opposite him. In the corner of the office a coal fire spat wood under a high heavy flame.

Lovely an warm in ere ayit, Michael said.

That it is. Ow was ya fust day?

Ar, went alright. I told ye about me other werk up Brownhills?

Ar. Tay too hard on ye already is it?

Ay that. I was told to leave the job.

Ow come?

Any assume they day want someone werkin two mines. They may think it possible for me to become an indrance. I ay sure ow they knew it.

An om supposin ye want longer shifts now?

If iss available. Any extra an od be very grateful.

See what I can do. Lawrence returned his head to the paper and stretched it out.

Thank ye, Michael said, and left.

He moved down the mine. Again he was stood next to Cain, who looked up at him with that smile and said, Hello again.

He nodded.

Ow be ya other work?

Sacked me.

Ya jokin!

Michael shook his head. As they undressed, the other men on the cage turned and sneered at them. Again the heat rose through him.

Doe blame um, if I be honest. A man cor work so.

Already they squeeze us for all our juice. A man cor be squeezed dry.

They waded through the pit bog. Chokedamp lingered. He looked to the vent where the children had surfaced the day before and saw nothing.

In their stall, the two men worked the face of the wall with their pickaxes. Beads of sweat ran along every part of them. They shovelled their pickings into the small skip that was pulled along the tunnel by the young boys and girls.

Where's their families? He day need any more encouraging to provide his own boy with school so as to spare him from this. There was less of it in his old job, or perchance he just saw less of it. Here he had any been two days and it was already tolling him.

The chokedamp mixed with lingering clouds of soot forced them to stop every so often and cough their lungs up.

Michael heard the men in the next stall talking. He accosted them.

Ye can speak it to me directly.

The two men, both smaller and older than him, looked surprised, and then to each other and then back at him again. One was fat, and one thin.

We just wondered why they always put the new lads together is all, the fat one said.

It would make more sense to ave a new un with a more experienced hewer, the thin one said.

Cain's head protruded from behind Michael's shoulder. In this tiny space it looked as though it was stuck.

Ye think we doin a shit job do ye?

Not at all.

Iss just.

Mind yown. Come on Michael.

And they went back to their stall and attacked the face of it with more vigour than before.

Day tell me yowm new as well, Michael said.

Bin here close to a month now.

Where frum?

East Wales.

But ye spake—

Am Dudley born and bred. Moved west before comin ere.

Why not back to Dudley?

Sick of it.

Why?

Pack it in will ye, Cain hissed. He stopped picking to cough and then looked at him. Less juss get on wi it.

He returned his pickaxe to the wall.

V

THEN came the days of asking. The days of offering. The days of pleading. He aimed to waylay three colliery managers a day. He managed only one. Sometimes none. First were the other collieries in and around the village, of which there were three in total. He day hide the fact he worked already for fear that his dishonesty had lost him his job at Brownhills. No. No room for men needing extra work, no room for tired men.

He walked for sometimes eight miles a time through the smoke and chill of the night. He travelled to Bloxwich, to Goscote, to Wyrley, to Walsall Wood. No. Most collieries would not take him on for fear of him shirking. Some wanted him for longer shifts than he could offer.

His shifts grew no longer at Pelsall and so now he

visited Lawrence almost daily. No. His travels added only more time onto his daily exertion, and regularly he came home more exhausted than the other miners.

Meanwhile, Jane washed the boy's best clothes ready for school, only for him to struggle to get the shirt over his head. Michael had scarce time to fish, he could not afford bread and they ate potato and leek soup once a day.

Night. He washed lazily before slipping under the woollen blankets. Jane was knitting by candlelight. She took not an eye from her work.

Well? she said.

Can ye let it alone.

He starts school on Monday.

Ar.

Then she stopped working and looked down at him. We shan't be able to afford all he needs. He needs new clothes. He needs provisions. We had barely bin able to get by when he was a babby an he grows so fast. Whatull be next? Books, equipment… as well as more of him to feed.

Am tryin me bess.

I know, she said softly. Perchance it ay the best time for school.

He needs school. I woe ave him workin.

He needn't work but he needn't be schooled. Not right this moment, anyroad.

Find somethin, he said, turning over.

Bin thinkin it over. I can work, she said.

He shook his head. Nonsense. Nay.

If I can find work where om not forced on me legs all day, I can do it.

Who'll look after Luke? Who'll keep after the ouse?

I was juss thinkin.

Ye wanted a child. I needed a wife. Ye muss look after him. I cor do it an work all the time.

Needed a wife, she said venomously.

Ar.

Michael, yow needn't spell it in such harsh a manner.

He stared at the dark side of the room where Luke slept silently. Still want to tell him soon, he said. About his real mother.

I am his mother.

She blew out the candle and turned over. There they lay. At times like this he thought about Amelia. How different things would be if she was still there. He remembered everything about her but certain images more regularly prevailed over others. And these tended to be the oldest, when they were both still young. Thin fingers pulling at the cuffs of cardigan sleeves. Teeth gnawing an upper lip. Eyes squinting through sunlight over barleyfields. She in the chancel of the church stealing glances at him whilst singing. She at his bedside, undressing. Then he would remember who was actually beside him. He wondered if Jane regretted marrying him. It seemed to be the perfect solution for them in the beginning.

She came to the colliery on Friday. Met him outside the checkweighman's. The other men were eyeing her as she stood clean and washed with thin strands of hair blowing across her face.

Everythin alright? he said.

We need shoppin. She held out her hand for the payslip.

He passed it to her. Remember we need some in cash for the school fund.

She stared at the slip for a while. Nodded.

They went together to the payroll office and received most in scrip for the tommy shop and the rest in cash. It was enough for school but day leave much for food.

The tommy shop was a large cart on wheels. There was a long line outside. They joined the end of it. Two people inside the cart shuffled around and passed parcels of different provisions across to the workers. Everything was quiet. From the back of the line the workers in the shop could be heard clear above everything else.

At the front they got all they could afford. Leeks. Peas. Potatoes. Onions. A small parcel of grains. Compared to their old one, this shop offered smaller portions for more tokens.

The day before school, Michael went into the village. People flooded the streets after service. They moved in unison like some giant millipede. A few closed shops saw them coming and rushed to reopen.

He walked the opposite way, against the crowd. All of them in their best Sunday clothes. He in his ragged shirt. He struggled against the waves of people. Tired squinting eyes. The call of the fruit and vegetable salesman. The pipesmoke.

He bumped into a woman holding a little girl's hand. She wore a crystalwhite dress. He stared. Apologised. Walked. The sea of churchgoers subsided and he continued to the far end of the village, across the vast common lined with adolescent trees scarce of any leaves and the grass richly black.

He came upon the church where it sat embedded in the land behind a small cluster of bare pine trees. There were a few young people outside talking. They stopped to watch him as he approached. He looked at them and smiled quietly. They looked away.

Inside he saw the vicar tidying between the benches. He walked down the aisle and sat down. Here it was. The house of God with light of all colours coming through the windows. Told himself he woe come unless he had to. He had taken the halfday off to go there. The last chance for him was an empty building. As he turned to leave, the vicar popped his head up.

Michael. Ye juss missed service.

Ar. Sorry about that. An sorry I be ere not in me bess clobber.

Doe worry, the vicar said, rising with a small cushion in hand. After punching it he bent back down to replace it. What can I do ye for?

Guidance really. Possibly a praya.

The vicar stopped what he was doing and walked around the benches and sat next to him. Still surprised him how young he was, for a vicar. He looked not much older than Michael. Centre parted, smart hair. Clean-looking face with not many wrinkles. Bright blue eyes.

What guidance do ye seek?

Om tryin to send the little un to school. But we bin strugglin, moneywise. Of bin tryin to get more work, or longer shifts. Suppose om after some good luck.

Ye want the Lord to bestow good fortune upon ye?

Ar. Somethin like that.

He is not a charm of fortune, Michael.

Sorry. I mean to say, this is a bad time for us. A really bad time. Not sure what to do.

The vicar smiled and nodded calmly. It was a pitiful look. He put a hand on Michael's shoulder. That ye have come to Him in ya time of need proves enough ya relationship with Him. He will always try an help his children in need. Now, let us pray.

They knelt. The vicar swiftly without problem. Michael with lagged stiffness.

Creator God, said the vicar, please show your son Michael that you are here for him. Show him your love. Show him your everlasting greatness. He is struggling to deal with the situation his life deals him in this moment. Show him your righteous right hand. Allow him to draw strength from you. Through Jesus Christ our Lord, Amen.

Michael opened his eyes and glanced at the vicar. Was that it? he said.

The vicar turned to him and lifted himself up and looked down on him.

Yes, that is it.

Thank ye, he said, struggling to his feet.

Are ye in need of anything else, Michael?

No, hopefully that works. Michael smiled and nodded. He held out his hand. The vicar shook it quick and soft, whilst already turning back to the altar.

Do try to come to service. It saddens me to see ye here only in time of need.

One thing at a time, Michael said.

Father and son in the pond before sunset. Applegreen weeping willows broke their backs over the edges where dull birds loafed in groups and shouted at one another. The water rippled outwards as they waded through it.

They were holding small poles with wire attached along them. Every now and then, Michael waded a little further across the shallows, pulled the wire from the water, swung it outwards and watched it dive back down. Whenever he did so, Luke copied him, his line only travelling half a dozen feet in front.

They did this a load of times before they caught something. It was a roach the size of the boy's hand. He took it from the line and handed it to Luke, who held it steady across his two palms. Its red eye was still and empty. Then it thrashed and slipped from its captor's grasp and shot into the water.

No! Luke said, searching about below, armdeep.

Michael reached into the cloth sack attached at his waist, pulled out a worm and stuck it on the end of his line. Doe worry about it, son, he said. Ow about ye goo an find some more bait.

The boy dropped his pole and turned to walk away.

Tek ya rod.

He watched the boy go, wondering the whole time if he actually enjoyed fishing, fetching bait, or catching frogs for fun, or lying in the long grass on the common and listening to the chirp of the crickets, or watching hunting foxes spring nosefirst into the feet of hedgerows.

That night they roasted two small roach over coals. Jane cooked a vegetable gravy and boiled potatoes to go with them. Michael watched Luke as he tentatively pulled the flesh back on the fish with his teeth, the fingers of steam reaching upwards. Two measly roach and his prayer. It was worth taking half the day off.

School tomorrow. He tried to view it with excitement and push to the back of his mind the worries of how they would afford it.

VI

THE stall they worked on was starting to deepen. There was more room to move around and more space for the carts and tubs to carry the burrowed earth and coal away. The blokes in the next stall stopped questioning when they realised their own stall was less broken in.

The pair on stall five had hewed large swathes of sharp crude coal for the past three days. Michael day know Cain's motive but he matched the double effort he had been employing. They picked so much that soon their feet were buried in lumps of coal. They started finding it difficult to shovel and so set about clearing it before picking more. He needed to earn enough so they could eat well on tokens and still have enough for the school fees. He held steel determination in his eyes, in his hands and arms. He was seethingly angry at the wall of coal and set about murdering it.

Let me tek ye for a pint after shift's end, Cain said, showing that crooked brown smile.

Gorra get back, he replied.

Iss on me. I ave somethin I need to run by ye.

Michael wiped the sweat from his forehead with the back of his arm and straightened his back and sighed. Alright, he said, sticking his shovel in. He avoided looking back at the boy that dragged the coal cart.

A thunderous crash came from the neighbouring stall. Followed by a hiss. Michael and Cain stopped picking. They looked at each other and in that moment they both knew. Only one thing made such a vile sound in the pits. It was malevolent and shadowy and true. And it comes and goes in a flash. Take one look and die.

They lifted their lamps and walked round to the next stall. Held them up. Dust and soot fell all around. Only dark clouds visible. They lifted sleeves to their chins. After a moment the dust settled and the lamplight shot through in beams like some miniature lighthouses. Only blackness still. The blokes who worked this stall were missing. Only a sad heap of dark rubble reaching from floor to ceiling remained. Coal and clay and stone. A few other men appeared, stuffed into the small passageway holding their lamps. Nobody spoke.

They fetched the undermanager. He stood silently in the tunnel for half a minute, as if he were doing some mental calculations. Dig them out, he said, and walked away.

When a lad came with a skip, Cain shouted at him. Get our skip, not that one. Stall five.

The lad said something under his breath and went away. Michael stopped shovelling.

Doe look at me like that, Cain said. Weem the ones clearin. May as well get paid for it.

After ten minutes they found bits and pieces sticking out of the rubble. A thin black arm. A rag of torn trouserleg. It was an hour before they fully recovered the men and laid them flat out next to one another. The bodies were loaded onto skips and pushed down the tunnel and through the pitfloor, up the inbye and across the sump to the cage. As they did, each miner stopped picking and watched. It was silent save the dull scrape of the skip against the track, the slosh of the bog in the pitfloor as they waded through it. Some miners helped to push and pull the skips. Some sat eating their snap.

The undermanager went with the bodies up the cage. Back to work, he shouted.

However much Michael day like their workneighbours, he never did wish anything like that upon them. Or anyone. They day speak it to one another, but he and

Cain knew they had to be more careful. Needed to make sure they had enough support beams put up. They'd close stall six for a few days, then move new people in.

Poor bastards, he said.

Who? Cain replied.

Under a brassy moon, they were ushered outside by the landlord. The folks entering the pub looked them up and down.

Now juss ave a perch an ya pints shall be with ye afore ye can say Jack Robinson.

They were sat down at a rotting wooden bench and had a view of the golden light that shone through the window. There were children kneeling on the sills laughing.

Shall be avin a word wi this cunt soon as he brings our pints, Cain said.

Michael was too occupied watching the warmth radiating from inside. They wor wealthy. Poor, even. Most people in there were. Outside was cold. November weather.

The landlord day return. Instead came a young girl holding two glasses filled with brown ale. She set them down and turned to walk away.

Where's the landlord? Cain said.

Beyind the bar, the girl said.

Ow come weem sat out ere?

Most men wash afore they come is all.

Fuckin difference it mek?

Iss alright, Michael said. He smiled at the girl and thanked her and she went back inside.

Tay alright.

Served us day they. What did ye want to talk about?

They sipped at their drinks and rubbed their hands together and held them to their mouths and blew.

Get to it. Doin a good job on that wall ay we? Cain said.

Ar. Suppose.

Ye doe say much do ye?

Suppose not.

People judge if a man doe say much then he mussn't think much. I reckon thass a dangerous idea to hold.

Michael nodded. Gulped his ale. So why were ye sick of Dudley?

Cain throated a massive portion of his drink and winced. He beat his chest and belched. History ayit. Yowm born an bred round ere?

Ar. Brownhills. But I worked an lived in Pelsall in the past. Got laid off. Moved about a bit, but never far.

Ye never wish to run away?

Sometimes.

Whym we sat out here? I cor believe it. Landlord can forget about us payin.

This Michael cor disagree with. He had no money. He simply raised his glass to him and smiled.

Ow's ye boy gettin on at school?

Doe know. Bin there less than a wik.

Cain fixed his eyes firmly on Michael. His face stern. The blackness only disrupted with those piercing eyes. His upper lip alesoaked and shining. Right. Ye need money, do I lie?

Michael frowned at him. Who doe?

I may ave somethin. Ye need to swear this woe meet any ears other than yown. Not even the wife.

Goo on then.

I ay avin a loff.

I believe ye.

Cain glanced around the yard. Drew closer.

This lass month past, of bin workin as a resurrection man.

Michael moved back and frowned. Then he smiled and even laughed a bit. Raised the glass to his lips and looked at those eyes that still were stuck in him. He put the glass down.

Iss easy werk, Cain continued. Ye get em when theym fresh, so iss easy to transport em, so they woe fall apart.

Yowm jestin, surely?

No.

Ow did ye get into such a line a work?

Bloke I know. Middleman for some fancy medical testers.

Well. I doe know what to say to that.

Pay's fair. Iss pelf, but iss fair. Could do wi another worker. Think about it. Om gooin to take a piss. Cain lifted himself up after downing his remaining ale and walked inside the pub.

The skyline was starting to glow its harshest red now. The cold was numbing Michael's hands. He blew into them again, finished his glass and lifted himself up. How his legs ached him. He felt like his hinges needed oiling.

Inside the pub a commotion. Shouting of men. Crashing of glass. A lone scream. He peered into the doorway just as Cain returned with blood falling from his fingertips.

Less goo, he said.

He watched Cain brush his hands back and forth on his trouserleg and wondered about him. If he was troubled or not. Illtempered yes, queer yes, evil only He would know. It was cold outside and warm at home. He should return to food and family yet the thought wor an excitable one. And he illtempered yes, and cold yes, and if the prayer worked only He knew an all.

And what might Cain have done to the landlord. Probably just knocked his lights out.

VII

MICHAEL slipped his boots off at the door. Left his scrip pay on the sidetable. Nobody was in there. He lifted the lid off a pot that was frothing from the mouth. The steam enveloped his face and moved around it in plumes. Weak and odourless like boiling water yet off yellow in colour.

Jane, he shouted.

She was sitting over Luke in the bed with a flannel to his forehead.

He's sick.

What is it?

Ay sure. He's feverish.

Michael sat down beside her at the end of the bed. The boy was flushed red. He had thin slashes lengthways on his hands. Michael held them in his.

Woe say what he did to get them, Jane said.

Oll ask him in the morra. Food's spillin over in there.

She got up and went to the kitchen. He sat there and watched Luke sleep until she called him.

They sat next to each other at the small kitchen table. It rocked when they left their elbow weight on it. She spooned the soup delicately to her lips. He shovelled it.

Sorry, iss the bess I could do, she said.

Doe be saft. Oll ave to goo fishin again soon.

She lifted the brown cruse with both hands and poured more soup into his bowl.

After finishing his meal, he leaned back with one elbow over his chair. Bin meanin to say.

Yes? she said, smiling. It was that smile she always wore and it day change.

I want ye here.

Less not get into it.

Iss true.

Whether iss true or not. It doe matter.

Why?

She kicked her chair back. Her food unfinished. She brought up the bowls and took them to the sink. He turned to her and repeated his question.

If ya got holes in ya socks, juss sew them an get on with it.

What? he said.

She stood and stared at the rain pelting against the back window. It sounded like a thousand fingers tapping.

That night he sat up watching the fire and watching the boy. It was always quiet in the early hours save the nocturnal whispers of the world. The spit and crackle of the fire. The lonely call of an owl. The muffled thrum of the wind that came down the chimney.

The fourth time he entered the room to check on Luke, he was awake. Through the doorway the letterbox of light revealed the wet of his eyes. Michael sat down and placed a hand on his foot. The old wooden bedslats creaked like a broken tree.

Ow ye feelin?

The boy sniffed and held his palm to his forehead. Hot. An sometimes cold, he said.

Michael placed his knuckles against the boy's forehead, and then his palm, and then his knuckles again.

Ye doe feel too bad. Should be alright for school in the morra.

The boy furiously shook his head. I feel really bad.

Weyull see.

Father.

Yes?

Luke sunk further down his bed. The slats moaning again.

Do I ave to goo to school?

Ar. Ye want to learn doe ya?

But.

What did ye do to get the cane?

Nothin.

Nothin? Ye must a done somethin.

Luke was silent.

Oll sort it. Doe worry. He pressed the boy's hair down either side of his head. Get to sleep, he said.

Luke must hate school. He worked his jaw thinking about the cane over Luke's hands. He was any a nipper. Is there anywhere they can be rid of the whip?

The clink and clatter of kitchenware. The fire dead. A thin film of cold on his arms and face.

Mornin, Jane said, without looking at him.

Michael took a deep breath and rubbed his face. The smell of earthsoaked hands. Bess get gooin, he said, rising from the chair and walking to the kitchen.

Shall keep Luke at hum today, she said.

What? Nay. Nay. I was watchin after him lass night. Nothin wrung with him. Said he felt the fever but he was fine. Fine, he was.

One day woe hurt him.

Bin there less than a wik. He's mekkin a fool of ye.

He ay. Yow sin his hands.

Michael took a glass of water from the table and drank. Ar. Oll sort that out.

How?

Oll ave a word wi the teacher. Juss goo. Goo check on him as he kips. He's fine. Yowll see.

I was checkin on him as yow was off doin God knows yesterdy. He was feverish.

God knows what. Went for one drink. Of bin tryin to set im up with school. So he woe ave to be doin what I ave me ole life.

She looked down. Did yow goo to school?

Ye know I day.

So how can yow know? It can be a frightnin place for a young child, she said calmly, eyes still down.

Frightnin place. Nothin compared to the bloody… His speech trailed off into a mumble. Bloody mines, was what he wanted to say. Instead he bent down slowly to pull on his boots and said, Juss mek sure he gets to school.

VIII

LAWRENCE lifted his head up from his newspaper. Seeing it was Michael, he turned to the side and exhaled.

Can work the nightshift if ye want. Pays a bit better. Any because the bloke who works ya stall on nights is very ill. Tuberculosis they reckon.

Thank ye very much, he said, and turned for the door.

Oh, an Michael? Doe tell a soul about it. Doe want a load a workers in ere after extra work.

He nodded and thanked Lawrence again and left.

Outside it had started to rain. And so with haste he made for the pithead and waited for his shift.

The bankswoman worked her job unloading. A skip fell to the floor, leaving its innards spilled out. She bent down with her left arm on her lower back and used her right to replace the coal. Dragged the skip to the loading cart and slowly squatted onto the black floor. Wrapped her arms around the skip and dug her fingers under it and grumbled and lifted it onto the loading cart.

People started appearing around the cage. God's spit drenched everything. They talked amongst themselves about the weather. One of them rejoiced and others shouted at him. Cain appeared, almost as if he was always standing there.

Thought about me job offer?

Honestly, no.

He had thought about it. And the more he dwelt, the more he saw it as possible divine intervention. Perchance that was how the Lord was answering the prayer. Then he was offered more decent, honest work, and realised it wor.

They stepped onto the cage. The talk amongst the men fell away. The noise of the working colliery almost drowned out by the rain. The wind battered it against their heads. The cage moved down the gullet of the mine. The first time they all seemed pleased to be going down and the heat burying them.

At their stall they could walk around with more room than in the tunnel, the sump, or even the inbye. He was imagining the sort of money obtainable for double the work.

They peeled the coal like layers of an onion. In between them stuffings of clay and mud that formed mounds the hewers used as restbenches. They had fitted more wooden beams along the sides of the stall to support the new openings.

Recently it seemed good coal was, for the most part, along the seam of the upper wall and the roof. They hacked at it. Dust and lumps of clay and soil fell into their squinting faces. They found themselves picking their eyes with bits of wetted cotton rag. The coal itself whacked them. One decently sized lump of rock came down on Cain's nose. He walked off ranting and raving. Michael hid his smirk.

At shift's end everyone at the inbye collected their clothes. Michael stayed behind. The nightworkers unloaded from the cage. As the dayworkers replaced them, Cain turned to him. Comin?

No.

Cain stopped and walked through the crowd back to him. Come on, he said, nodding to the cage.

Am on the next shift, Michael said.

Yow am?

Ar. Bloke on nights is sick.

Cain smiled wryly. Took his eye off Michael and nodded. See ya in the mornin then.

Then Michael realised. By nightshift's end it would be early morning, and time for the dayshift again. He felt a dry scratching in his throat. Coughed lightly.

He waited. The young boys and girls squoze out of their shafts and ran to the cage. The undermanager was watching him with baleful eyes. He nodded. The undermanager looked away. The cracking of the chains as the cage lifted up. The nightworkers milled about.

To ya stalls! the undermanager said.

Who's on five? Michael shouted to him.

He was ignored. He took his shirt from the floor and wiped the sweat off his head and neck.

Five?

It came from a bald man standing against the support beam removing his trousers.

He nodded. Name's Michael.

Bill, the man said, fetching a pickaxe from the bucket.

Ow's ya stallmate?

He's dead. Shall we? Bill smiled a friendly, welcoming smile.

It wor any different work at night. Everything was exactly the same. Bill worked slower than he or Cain but took less breaks. He coughed less an all. It seemed as though he was happier in general. He whistled and hummed as he picked.

We bin workin the ceilin today, Michael said.

On nights we doe tend to mess about up there.

Ar. Think it was juss we fancied more headroom.

Bill laughed. They carried on picking. The wicks from their Davy lamps wilted when gas passed through them. They projected onto the pantherblack walls. The light tinged them bourbon.

Michael picked hard into the wall, separating a large section of coal that showed itself through cracks that ran down to the floor and formed the shape of a foxglove bud. He lifted the light to it and examined it slowly. Replaced the lamp. Drew down hard onto the wall. And again. Returned to his inspection. The foxglove bud portion of coal was huge and separated more prominently now. He left the light on it and drew his axe again, hitting it flush in the centre. It split along the middle. A further flurry of strikes took it totally apart and it fell to the floor. A heap of powdery coal.

He had made a crater deep enough to fit the full of his hand. When bending down to shovel the lumps he noticed inside the wall a small fleck of shine. It reflected off the lamplight. He fingered it. The black from his hands dulled its glint. He got the lamp and held it closer to the wall. With his free hand he lightly chipped away at the rock around the flecked reflection. It trailed like veins under the surface.

He replaced his lamp on the floor once more and pulled the axe back and hit three measured strikes around the shine. It fell to the floor. Kneeling, he fished around the rubble and spat on it and took a damp bit of cloth and rubbed away the soot and dirt. A scrap of yellow gold the size of a shirt button. He halfgasped and started to cough. Quickly wrapped it in the cloth and slid it into his boot.

Bill was still hard at work on the other side of the stall.

Michael held the lamp to where he had found the nugget. It was shining still.

What ye gorpin at? Bill said.

He rose quickly and started picking at the coal above. Nothin. And when Bill continued picking, he scraped clayed dirt from the floor and pasted it over the shine.

Bill and the nightshift left up the cage. Michael remained. In between shifts he pissed against the tunnel wall. Coughed dark phlegm into cotton rags. Lay on the floor and looked at the gold. It caught the lamplight when he moved it tentatively in his filthy hands.

This was it. Everything he had been waiting for. He thought his luck was in when he was afforded extra work. Now he cor believe his luck. The Lord is not a charm of fortune, the vicar had said. More fool him now. This was everything. And there was more.

He set about mining as much as he could before the morning shift came down. There were men moving about and working, but in the hours between the main shifts the mine was plenty quieter. He could have spent this time topside, resting or even sleeping. But not after this.

After scraping away the paste he had covered the shine with, he realised the veins and fragments were deeper inlaid than he had first imagined. He had to work at separating the surrounding rock to bring the treasure to the fore.

About an hour later, as he was starting to break in the rock around the shine, carefully making sure not to damage any of it, the floor started to shake. Footsteps. Echoed grumbling. The men walked past. He watched and nodded to a few of them. Cain came last. He looked surprised.

Ye wor jestin then!

Michael shook his head.

An yowm fit for purpose?

Fit as a fiddle, me. Michael leant a sly eye towards the shine and then stepped in front of it.

Cain laughed. Bess get to it then. If ye need a brek juss tek it. Bin out all night meself. Could do wi a few breks an all.

Michael was still looking at him. Had been for a while. Could he trust him? No. But what else could he do? It would be impossible to hide what he was doing.

So he held the stare on his stallmate. Took Cain a bit to realise it. Eventually he stopped picking and stared back. His face already wet with sweat and lit a dim red.

What? he said.

Look.

Michael stepped aside, and left free and protruding was the bulbous growth of rock, chipped away at its border, veining and clumping with golden reflections.

Cain frowned and moved towards it and knelt. Wait, he whispered, and scrambled for his lamp and held it on the rockface. Ya jestin. Gold? He looked at Michael and frowned. Only his warmly lit bust visible in the darkness.

Certainly looks like it, Michael said, and he started to laugh. Cain grabbed him by the shoulder and smiled.

They concentrated their blows around the gleam. Working in tandem. They hit a rhythmic knock onto the wall. Each of them striking the exact moment after the other. They broke off the heap of coal that within it had golden veins. Then with chisel and hammer they broke apart the smaller pieces and started to form a parcel.

Individually they worked the gold out of the lumps. It was a delicate job. They had to try and keep good pieces as joined together as possible.

Cain went to the inbye and returned with his shirt and they placed their treasure inside. They took hardly any breaks. Michael was so exhausted his body became numb. His eyes so heavy with tiredness and the sweltering heat sapping the last of his energy.

He day want a partner on this. But at least this way, Michael woe have had to keel over to mine all of the treasure. As much as he day like Cain, he respected the man's work ethic.

By the time there was a few handfuls' worth, the wall turned clay and black again. They wrapped the shirt. They were boneweary. They said not a word for fear of neighbouring stallworkers with pricked ears.

At shift's end they left the mine as usual. Cain held his heavy balled shirt against his hip. Michael stumbled across the bank, his legs like giant lead weights. He heaved and retched coughs that sounded like the cries of a trapped animal.

At the edge of the colliery the two men leaned against a dilapidated stone wall. In the near distance now the lanterns that threw light on the colliery. He had forgotten what day it was, what time it was. Everything was dark, and seemed like it always had been.

Cain unfurled the shirt. There they sat. Glimmering in the glow yet dull still. The reflections casting small shapes subtly onto their faces.

Pawner closed by this time, Cain said. Less one of us tek em for now. We can split it in the morra when we've daylight. Or juss tek em to the pawner together. Let me tek em. Oll clean em up nice an all.

Iss me who fount em. Any fair I tek em for the night.

Cain looked at him and day speak. It was that look paired with silence that suggested doubt. Sure? he said.

Ar, Michael said, rubbing his forehead with the back of his wrist. He swayed lightly. His knees shook.

Goo on en. Puttin me trust in ye, Michael.

They transferred the metal from shirt to cloth rag. The new parcel placed under his arm. They shook hands firmly. Michael's knees buckled and he almost fell over.

Ye sure ye can mek it back alright?

Om fine, he said, and stumbled away.

IX

THE house was softly lit. He stepped in. Instantly a slap in his face.

Michael Luke Cash, Jane shouted. I was worried sick.

Allow me in the door fust, he said, holding his face.

He released his feet from the boots that seemed welded on. Fell against the door. Held his hands to his knees. Pushed his hair back behind his ears. Then collapsed.

She sighed and knelt and held him by the shoulders. Her brows lifted. Her mouth held open and her eyes scanned all about him. What on earth. What happened?

Eventually she sat him by the fire and removed his filthy wet clothes. Luke stood watching from the bedroom doorway. Michael ranted and raved at her to bring a pail of water. She warmed it on the fire. He demanded she light more candles. All the while he writhed about slowly on the floor like a worm.

When the water began to simmer he said, Thass enough, and ordered Luke to retrieve the parcel that had fallen beside his boots. The boy ran to the door. He stood there clutching the parcel in his arms, wet but wrapped tightly in cotton rag.

Iss heavy. What is it? Luke said.

Chop chop. Tek it to her, his father said.

Luke did so and stood watching. His eyes big and shining like those of a dog.

Empty it, Michael said.

Jane opened the parcel and dropped its contents into the water. Michael had stopped squirming now, but a wheezing cough peppered his breathing. Still he lay on his back, sweating profusely. His head stuck upward and his eyes fixed on the bucket. Eyes which looked mad like those of some awful beast's being cornered by a hunter.

Wash it, he said.

She moved her hands around the bucket, frowning at him. What is this?

Jane continued. The water turned black.

Where yow bin? she said. Over a day yowve bin gone.

He let his head fall onto the floor again and sighed deeply. He spoke with breathy gaps. Worked a triple shift. Thass more money. We need.

Yow cor have warned me?

Ow's that lookin.

Black.

He coughed hard and long. It became a fit. She leant over him and patted his back firmly. He eked out a word. Strain.

She took the strainer from the beam near the fire and placed it over a larger pail. Then she sent the water through it. Left behind were flecks of dazzling light, small bundles of coal. Some chunks, some scraps.

What is it? Luke said.

Jane looked down. Then back at him. Michael, what is this?

What is it? Luke said.

Whass it look like.

She got up and fetched a candle and placed it on the floor. Then another. And another. She built almost a tiny shrine whereupon they worshipped this newborn light. All that it held. Wealth. Change. Life. She on her knees fell backwards and held a hand to her chest.

Where frum?

The mine.

What is it? Luke said.

Michael was sat up against a chair now. Iss school for ye, son. Better clobber. Ow's pork chops sound?

Well why on earth did yow goo on about more shifts

when yow had this? she said, letting out a sigh closely followed by a laugh.

His body forced a gravelly screech through his throat. It went on and on until he retched up a thimblesized nugget of bile. He struggled to speak. Well… thass why I. Was gone so.

What dyow think iss worth?

Bring it ere, he said.

She shuffled over to him. He filtered his fingers through the bundle of metal. Some of the pieces jagged and interlaced with coal. Some of them shining and pure. Some of them trapped in harder grey rock. He breathed heavily. Picked up the largest piece that was about the size of a ball bearing. His eyes fell tears. She looked down at him and held him in her arms.

Less get yow to bed, she said, yowm knackered. Still be here when yow wake.

He looked at the piece of gold and said, without taking his eyes from it, Oll sleep ere.

X

JANE was dragging him to bed the next morning. Her dress damp from where she supported him. He collapsed onto the bed. Simultaneously radiating heat, dripping wet and trembling. He frowned with eyes closed. Work…

She pulled the quilts up to his chin as he writhed slowly in the bed. Yowll need to miss it today. Yow cor work in this state. Especially after sittin up out the front all night. She got up to leave and he threw the quilts.

Boilin… iss boilin…

He felt her lean over him and pull the quilts up to his chest. Opened his eyes. She raised her brows and looked down at him. Pulled her mouth in tight on one side, forming a dimple. He felt beads of sweat down the groove of his skull. His teeth chattering and grinding coarsely like coal skips on the track. He coughed and coughed and coughed.

Doe worry, she said, be restful. Rest.

Luke came in. Is he alright? he said.

Yes, now goo an out. And as he left she shouted, Fetch a pail a water an—

The back door swung open. The cold mauled them. He shivered. She turned. Shouted about letting the heat out. The back door slammed. Luke came carrying a dripping pail and dropped it next to her.

The flannel, she said.

When it was given to her, this small greystained flannel, she plunged it into the water and rung it out and dabbed it slowly onto Michael's head.

Then he closed his eyes tightly. Took deep rasping breaths. Inhale. Exhale. The whistle of the draught through the window, the clamour of crows outside of it, Jane comforting him with soft words and hums, fading… fading… gone.

upon the precipice of a giant slagheap and around the top a halo of white broke open the broiling red cloud and ravens and crows and rooks and hooded gulls flew in medleys of quiet, their beaks wide and malevolent and mocking yet muted, and amongst the slagheap dead trees bloomed from the blackness

And below coagulated cuts of black water surged

And he was breaking open a tree and out of it flowed liquid gold and it ran along his hands that were black as day and it shone bright as the light that led him down the slagheap and in the water where his skin became bright white

And in his palm the gold

And over in betwixt two cuts of water he stood looking down at a fallen earth that held children all looking up to him from their darkness with bright shining eyes

And he held the gold

And all around him giant slagheaps tumbled coal in great landslides and lightning hit the birds that befell the land ablaze, each of them circling and burning. And the child Luke below with pickaxe

She drew the flannel down his temple and tutted.

He swallowed and looked around the room. Time is it? he said.

About midday.

Luke? He readjusted himself slightly so he was on his side and facing her directly.

Off to school.

I day spake to his teacher about them lashes.

Doe yow worry about anythin. There'll be soup for later. Try and get some more sleep.

She wrung out the flannel again and touched his forehead with the back of her hand. He coughed. A quickly worsening cough that caught and caught. He hunched over retching and it sounded as though he had grit in his throat. She patted and rubbed his back, soothing him. On the bed he left small pools of black spit. She held a little metal cup of water to his mouth and he sipped it. It fell and stuck along his throat and he held in an instinctual cough. Gurgling. Swallow.

Bess get back to kip now, she said.

He grunted. Rolled over slowly. She pulled the quilts up to his shoulder and tucked them around him. Her hands following the winding curve of his body.

He opened his eyes. The bedroom door was closed but all the sounds of the house were still open to his ears.

Yes, thank you, that shall be nice, a lowtoned voice said.

The voice of Jane responded. Wait a moment, iss down the well outside.

Footsteps. The opening and closing of a door. A sigh. Sinking of the fireside chair. A low whistling. He lay on his side. He was drenched and the bed soaked through.

He stayed facing the window with his eyes in the top corner of their sockets. Shuffled steps got louder before the closing of a door.

Thank you ever so much.

Never yow mind.

Chickens out the back as well?

No, no. We had but a few once upon a time, but they wor good layas.

Pigs?

No.

Everything running in here?

Workin as it should. May I ask the business for ya showin up so unannounced?

A pause.

As you know your husband is no longer an employee of the Brownhills Colliery Company… Everything is written there.

A pause.

Five days?

I do apologise.

Only five days?

The wheeze of the fireside chair. Footsteps. Clink of a glass.

How am a family supposed to…

I do apologise, madam. Thank you for the water.

More footsteps. Opening of the front door.

Good day.

Silence. Michael closed his eyes.

watching a small boy pull a coal skip the size of a train carriage

And so tiny was the child dragging his fingers deeply into soil and pulling but moving nowhere holding his head down and slipping on grooves formed in the earth each few steps regaining his stance and digging his hands in and falling still facefirst in the black

And he was next to the boy and unlatching his chains and lifting his head up and a clean face, the face of his father, fixed blue eyes on him pure and smooth

Scratched sweeps along the wooden floor. He rolled over. Jane pulled a long straw broom about the room. She had her back to him.

Ye ave to do that now?

Yes, she said, without turning or stopping.

Time is it?

Almost fowah.

He slowly lifted himself up and shuffled to the edge of the bed. Put his feet down on the wooden floor. Bits stuck to his feet.

Who was in the ouse earlier?

She turned and laid the broom against the doorframe. Someone frum ya old work.

Whass he after?

They want the house back. Since yowm no longer workin there.

Oll goo an sort it, he said, rising and stumbling and falling again all in one motion.

She rushed to him. Knelt. Lifted him up. Nonsense, she said. Yow need to rest all day. Oll goo to Pelsall, see what they have. She put him back to bed and lifted the covers. He coughed and coughed again, breathing labouredly.

Ye sure, he said.

Yes. Yes. I can goo to the shop an fetch Luke on me way back an all.

Oll be up shortly. Meet ye in the village.

Doe worry. Yow juss need some rest. More sleep if anythin. What use am yow in this state.

She left. He stretched out along the bed and pulled the blanket up to his face. The ceiling was made of thin wooden slats that sometimes leaked water. He was watching the swollen patterns of the wood, where it was aged, where it showed scars. He followed the lines and curves that formed into circular cloudlike balls and drifted back to sleep.

◆

floating on his back in calm water and everything blurred. And about the air a sweltering heat and the reek of choke-damp that smelled like some awful earthy gas

He noticed he was naked and the water all about him black and boiling

And above the cutline a wave of boiled blue sky hazed a figure, a small figure that came walking to the bank of the cut and wearing a black padded coat unzipped to show multiple layers of cardigan that stretched so it appeared like the disembowelled belly of a fish

It was Luke at the bank of the cut and he, Michael, was shouting

And Luke stepped into the water and Michael thrashing at the

He woke to the call of an owl. A thin beam of light poked around the doorframe. He swallowed. Rose from his bed. His shirt damp and cold. Jane was sat at the table with a pair of shoes. One lifted up to her chest, the sole coming away from it.

She turned to him. Her face beamed in unsteady candlelight. Her shadow lunged across the wall then back again. She fumbled them away from the table and got up and walked to the fire where the pot was rumbling.

Feelin better? she said.

Michael looked across at the table where she had stood before he came in, and then back towards where she stood now. Ar, a bit. What ye doin?

She moved around the pot and then to the kitchen and made herself look busy. Tea obviously, she said.

He looked back at the table. Below it dimly visible the bundled sack with the black objects lying on top. He walked slowly over to the table. Grabbed the chair. Fell onto it. Sighed.

She came and held her hand to his forehead.

Luke burst through the back door. Juss sin a whammel outside! He stopped and held his hands together. His head down.

He come out a school smilin, Jane said softly. Reckon he's got a few mates now.

Said I would sort that teacher, day I? Michael said, running his hand over his scalp and scratching.

Needn't, she said triumphantly. I spoke to him. Luke was misbehavin is all.

Still day change things. He hated to see it, but it was done now. The boy did look happier, even after he had quelled his excitement upon spotting his poorly father.

What kind a whammel? Michael said.

Luke's eyes lit up. A terrier! Can we get one?

Well. There's loads a terriers, what sort?

Luke searched the silent room for answers.

His father mucked in. Irish, Bull, Staffy…

It was juss a terrier.

Michael nodded. Juss a terrier.

Luke was the spit of Amelia. Whenever Michael saw him, he saw her. How his chin was dimpled, how his eyes were bright blue. If only she could have seen. It made him want to tell the boy she had indeed existed and how much they looked alike. Always he was debating in his mind whether it was the right thing to do. To both Jane and the boy, their relationship was that of mother and son. How could a few words change that? Perhaps the knowledge that the boy had carried his true mother off would cause more harm than good anyway. But when Michael saw Jane, he day see the boy's mother.

Jane brought over three bowls one after another, smiling as she did.

He felt his eyes widen, his heart quicken, and turned to her. Where is it? he said.

She nodded to the kitchen drawer that usually held needles and wool.

Was supposed to be took to the pawner today. He brushed his hand over his head. Oh, and the mine. The mine. There might be more.

The mine can wait, she said. Yow need to get well. Am sure Cain will bring good news in the morra. Will yow be fit for work then?

Believe so. Doe feel too bad.

She held a hand to her chest and blew on her soup, swallowed it and looked at Michael. Her face in shadow. Ay gonna ask how I got on, about the new lodgins?

New lodgins? Luke said.

She spoke in a higher inflection, as she always did to Luke. Yes. Weem movin. Ay that excitin?

Ye spoke to them at the mine? Michael said.

Theym lookin into it. Hopefully they've somewhere for us. Weem on the list anyroad.

Things am lookin up then, Michael said.

They shared an uneasy look. They both knew that could mean anything. The amount of labourers coming in and out of the village and its different mines and works, that list could be endless.

Luke put his finger to his mouth. Will I stop gooin to school?

Nay son. Ye ay gettin out of it that easy.

XI

He woke to whispers. A closing door. The light around the doorframe was quieter. He was far less feverish now, but exhausted still. He day move. His eyes were pulled wide open. The whispers continued. That unmistakable sigh of the fireside chair. The voices still hidden. Their constant hiss still incessant.

Luke was fast asleep. It sounded to him like the voice of a man. He rose out of bed and toed across and placed an eye in between the door and frame.

Again, I apologise about the lateness, Cain said, sat low and relaxed in the fireside chair.

Nay, nay. Juss bess not to wek him. Yowll want him ready for work tomorrow.

Of course.

Would yow like some a the soup, we have a bit left over.

That would be lovely.

She moved across the room. Michael's eye stayed on Cain. Watching the man watching her. She handed Cain a bowl and spoon. He sat eating it without speaking for a while. And then he said, Fine fittle, this.

She thanked him.

Silence.

Cain moved forwards in the chair. It growled as he shifted his weight. Jane's seated shadow drew back.

What is it ye do? Werk?

No. I cor stand for very long without this leg givin me bother.

Whass wrung wi it?

In another life, she said, it was broken rather badly. Well, that an me hip, but iss the leg still bothers me.

Cor ye get ousewerk, werk where ye can sit for all ya pleasure?

She was silent for a moment.

Yes. I can.

Well woe he be appy about ye earnin towards the pot?

He doe want me troubled. What wi me leg. An he knows Luke has bin a handful most of his years.

He nodded. Ow I miss me boy, he said, his voice formed sympathetically.

Got one a yown?

Ar. Back in Wales. Life's easier on me own. But it gess lonely.

Why doe yow goo back to him?

Woe know me now. Iss already done. Lose all father an life gets easier. But a course Michael could never.

I juss think his pride can overpower, sometimes. Truth is Luke is needin less an less as each day passes, an all.

He held out a hand and placed it on her figure. Michael gripped the door handle.

Ye muss a bin worried sick about him.

She pulled her arm from under his hand. What was it yow wanted me to tell him?

He took his hand away. Ar wondah, he said, his gapped smirk visible, shifting in the feeble light. Ar wondah if he told ye about what we fount, our lass shift.

Tells me everythin.

Cain slouched back into the seat again. It gasped. He nodded. Well, ye can understand me worry when he day show up for werk this morn. We was supposed to be gooin to the pawner fust thing. I thought he an ye had tekken an gone. He spoke louder now. Ar fount that stuff juss as much as he. An today I had double the werk, they day provide me a stallmate.

I apologise, she whispered.

Michael opened the door and stood watching them.

Her figure turned to him. Cain's wet eyes shifted independently from his head and the rest of his body.

Whass gooin on, Michael said.

She got up. Sorry, we was too loud. Ow yow feelin?

Fine. What ye doin ere?

Sorry I was too loud, Cain said, smiling.

Iss no bother.

Michael walked across the room and after a pause Cain got up, almost sprang up. Yam, he said, ave this seat.

Nay. Bin on me arse all day.

Cain nodded and sat back down. Michael stood awkwardly close to him and continued, What do ye want?

Juss thought od pop in an check on ye.

Am alright. Shall be returnin to werk in the morra. The stall?

Cain cast his eye across to Jane, who still stood there. Michael told him she could hear whatever news he had.

Struck no more today. Just coal, an most of it slack an all.

Reckon we got it all?

Nay. If iss there iss there. Muss be more of it.

Michael turned to Jane and asked her to fetch the parcel. They sat around the table together and watched silently as Jane opened it. The golden shine dulled by darkness. In this limited candlelight the gold looked brassy and slight. A minor bit of scrap.

Can tek it to the pawner tomorra, Cain said. Before werk.

Ar.

We get two thirds of it, Jane said.

Cain frowned, turned to Michael. We fount that together. Ye needed me to get it out. Far as I can see ye almost killed yaself with all that werk. We split it down the middle.

It was quiet for a moment. No sound save the wisp of candleflames.

I fount it, Michael said, an we need it for the lad's school. But ye did aid me in tekkin it out.

Sixty to forty then, Jane said.

Cain leant back in the chair and smiled wryly. Fine then, he said.

Yowll need to be up early, so off to bed, Jane said, closing the parcel. A shadow came across the wall. The hand on her wrist not her husband's.

Let me view it a bit longer.

Can look with all the day's light in the mornin, Jane hissed, pulling her arm away and the parcel with it. Cain watched her, straightfaced and stern as she went to the drawer.

Michael got up from the table and asked Cain if he had far to travel and he stared into the fire for a bit. He said he had quite a journey to his house. He said he had underestimated the distance between their lodgings and perchance it would be better if he stayed there for the night. They could go to the pawnshop in the morning from there. Michael denied him.

Cor blame me for tryin, Cain said, laughing. I apologise for me rudeness. Ternin up late. Wekkin ye up. Askin for a bed. Doe they say a good Christian never terns away a weary traveller? He laughed again in fake politeness. Any jestin. Goodnight to ye.

They watched him walk down the path and disappear into the darkness.

Two figures whispered in the dark.

If yow day trust him then why tell our address?

I day. I day tell him.

Well how does he know?

Ay the foggiest. Could be he went askin after I day show up for werk today.

What time will yow goo tomorra?

For God's sake, if ye ask me another question.

She rolled over in the bed. His eyes were full of moonlight.

Where did ye put it? he said.

In the drawer.

The one wi the lock?

Now who's askin all the questions.

He coughed coarsely into his sleeve. Night, he said.

Night.

Outside the moon slipped from his view now. The faint red horizon coloured the clouds yellow. The boy ground his teeth as he slept. Sometimes he would mumble. Tonight was just the coarse grinding, steady and rhythmic, as if it matched his heartbeat, as if following the lazy yellow clouds across the swollen sky.

Wake up, Jane said, pulling at his shirt.

The birds sang yet outside it was still dark. He rose swiftly and turned to her. She stared at him. Her face blurred.

I heard a bang, she said.

Outside the bedroom, movements. Another bang. He sprang from the bed and opened the door.

The heat hit his face and roared at him. Blazing orange fire spilled over the fireguard, swarmed the chair and shot up the curtains. The front door ajar and bent from its hinges. Rain spat into the entrance.

Get Luke! he shouted.

Jane bolted from behind him. She was holding Luke by the hand. Her crooked run outside. Michael grabbed the metal bucket and ran out aside her towards the well. He yanked the pump. It churned and screeched with each drive of his arm, but nothing came out. Jane went back into the house and returned with another pail, the one she used to wash clothes.

The pump ay werkin, he said, the rainwater streaming from his hair and into his eyes.

Tie the bucket, she shouted.

He grabbed the rope and looped it round the bucket handle and let it drop down the well. After a moment he pulled it back up. Luke stood under the gapped wooden porch that halfshielded him from the rain. The house was glowing bright and shone across the length of the small garden. The bucket came up overflowing. He held it by his side, his right shoulder dipping, and ran back inside.

The fire climbed higher and higher, up to the roof and swarming over the chair and spitting outwards towards the front door. He threw the bucket against the coals and sent it out instantly. It hissed angrily and sent a wave of air and rushing flame up the wall.

The chair was roaring and hot along the top, but the bottom was still. He bent down and brought it into his arms. Wincing and groaning, he pushed his legs upwards and lifted the chair and walked it to the doorway and threw it outside into the rain. It lolled over on its side and the flames were sent wildly about in the wind.

Still the wall was burning. It seeped up to the roof. Smoke impregnated the house. He held the crook of his elbow to his mouth and retched. Crossed Jane as she threw water at the wall. Again he ran outside and came back with a full bucket. Threw it against the wall.

Luke stood in the doorway, soaking wet and silent. For a while they lobbed water at the flames until they quietened and died out. Only clouds of smoke were left drifting around the room.

He stood over the drawer. It was broken and upturned on the floor. He looked at it but day reach for it. Jane had set up a few candles on the table and held a towel over Luke's head as he shivered.

Outside crows cried as daylight came. Four shrill shouts every measured moment. The wall blackened. The roof leaking water.

Must of bin him, Michael said, stood over the drawer again. He kept going back and forth between there and the leaking roof he had placed a bucket under.

What ya thinkin? Jane said.

He looked at her still sat with Luke to her chest, who had fallen asleep wrapped in the towel. Then went to the door and slipped on his boots.

All this time spent saving the house, Cain could be anywhere, he thought. The first place he checked was the pawnshop.

Someone was knockin on me door juss before openin, the pawner said. I dared not answer it for fear of burglars. It happens all too often in this business.

Anythin else? Day shout or say anythin?

Nothin else notewerthy.

Where's the nearest pawner from ere?

That would be Simmy.

He asked where exactly Simmy's was and the man obliged. He thanked him and left. It was already time for him to be on the way to work. Cain would pawn the gold as quick as he could, surely. Michael ran through the village and across the large commons that were like big ponds of sinking mud.

Upon reaching Simmy's, a coughing spasm sent him to his knees retching into the mud. A woman holding a basket of apples aside her waist stopped and bent down and asked if he was okay.

Where's the pawner?

She pointed him in the direction.

He went barging through the door spreading his filth and grime. The pawner behind the desk startled at the sight.

Anyone come in today? Michael shouted.

No. Yowm me fust customer today.

Michael groaned and let his head fall into his hands. The pawner's fright was eased at the sight.

But by the look a that fizzog yow ay got anythin wuff pawnin.

Michael lifted his head and squinted. Coughed into the palms of his hands. Stepped outside.

There has to be more of it. That's what Cain said, the same night he stole it. There has to be more of it. So why did he steal it? Because why werk for more when ye can juss tek the lot an goo. But he cor be far. No, he could be anywhere. In this country everything is close yet far, sparse yet dense.

He decided to go back to the mine and see for himself. He thought so an all that there had to be more of it.

What the fuck do ye look like? Lawrence said.

Michael stood in the office wetter and muddier than he had been in the pawnbroker's. Sorry for me lateness.

Lawrence looked at him with scared eyes, with eyes of pity, where he stood, filthy and soaking and hopeless.

Ye feelin better now?

Did ye replace me shift today?

Nay. We've an empty stall down there.

Empty?

Ar. That bastard Cain causes me more pain than ye.

Michael looked down at his feet. So he really was gone. Of course he wor down the pit.

Goo on then, yowm already beyind.

Michael opened the door.

Oh, an Michael. Forget about any more extra shifts. What did I say about not tellin a soul? An now I ave em all up here tellin me we afforded ye extra werk. Plus if iss doin this to ye, then od say om doin ye a favour. There's a reason we ave all these inspectors breathin down our necks.

He wanted to tell Lawrence about the children down there. And how the inspectors did nothing when they were bunged a pound. And how they were all dying and what does it matter how quickly they do it. Instead he left and descended the mine as the rain pummelled his back.

XII

INSIDE he removed all his clothes. The blokes that walked about the pit whistled and jeered at him. He ploughed through the water towards the tunnel.

Someone grabbed his shoulder. Michael turned and stared. The undermanager drew back. He told him he was late and what the fuck was he naked for and Michael without saying anything thrust his head forward and left him on the floor of the pit.

Ten times over. A hundred times over. For what seemed like a thousand times over he drew back and hit forth on the coalface. The soot built like black clouds around him. There had to be more.

His arms left the axe behind himself and he stooped over, holding his hands on his knees. He coughed and retched and vomited blackness. The sight of it shining in the lamplight was like the ghostly shimmer of the coal.

He lifted his head up and forced the light to view the coalface, up and down and left and right. Nothing but more glistening blackness. He sat there for the rest of his shift. Let his hands stop shaking. Slowed his breathing.

Inside it shines more than out. Cain knew there was no more of it down there. Why day God know? Doe He see everythin? If there's no more gold then Cain has it all. All of it and all there will be of it.

He re-dressed at end of shift. Heard someone clear their throat and looked up. It was the undermanager. He shot hot breath through his nostrils.

Be seein ye soon, lad. Really soon.

Got bigger problems than ye, Michael said.

Above ground he melted into the crowd of tired workers. They talked and laughed. One of them directed something towards Michael. He turned to them.

What?

I say ye gave that undermanager a good un. About time someone did.

The praising man was short and bald and had white pinpricks for eyes.

Ar, he's a right miserable un, another miner said.

Michael nodded to them and looked back ahead.

Fancy a pint? the bald man said.

Got to get back.

Another time then.

Ar. Good evenin.

Good evenin, the group shouted, some louder than others.

Michael along the cut. Sleet falling fast and sharp. The water pulsed and danced. Mallards and coots hid. From him or the weather he day know.

A muffled cry. He stopped. Listened. Again the voice. He turned. Down the cut under a bridge he had not long passed, a body thrashed about in the water. The body's head bobbed up and down. With it the gurgled cries.

His boots slipped along the bogged bank and wind pushed him backwards. His eyes worked to focus as the sleet streamed down his brow. Under the bridge it looked like a lad. He was thrashing still. Michael reached out and grabbed him. The lad gasped as he was pulled from the water.

Lad, Michael shouted. Oi lad, yowm safe. Iss alright. Iss fine.

The lad, upon realising where he was, calmed.

Cor ye swim?

The lad stared up at him with gaping eyes. They caught the light from the water that reflected the copper sky where burning furnaces stabbed through stormclouds.

Those eyes themselves like little pools of water. Under the bridge the crash of the sleet was softened. The lad coughed up chokes of water and spit.

Stay out a the water if ye cor swim, Michael said. He went walking into the sleet for a moment before turning back. Still the lad was lying there, clearing his throat.

Ay I sin ye before?

No, the lad said without eyeing him.

He had seen him before. On this cut. With a cut of his own behind the ear. It was raining then an all. Thunder and lightning.

Am ye homeless? Michael said.

He looked at Michael. Then down. Om alright, he said.

Ow old am ye?

Sixteen.

Michael turned around. The sky broiling and furious. The sleet raking across the cut. Ay no place to be out in this weather, he said. Come with me.

Swans pushed themselves down the canal and watched him. Then watched the lad some ten feet behind. Michael turned a few times and shouted, but the wind washed out his words. Water pushed against the bank. It spilled over the cut and brushed their ankles. Michael eyed the lad again and watched him amble along. He day forget seeing him. Bloodied ear. Lightning. The rainy cut. Perchance he was an urchin, or a runaway.

Narrowboats carrying goods came along, almost sinking in the cut. Men stood aboard throwing buckets of black swill out either side. Possibly it was a flood to end all floods. Possibly this village would be swept up in the rains and drowned. What use would it all be then?

Inside the house, Jane stood over Luke at the table with her hand on his shoulder. She turned to them as they came through the door. What an earth, she said.

Fetch some towels, Michael said.

Luke craned his neck around Jane. Who's that, Father?

Juss goo.

Luke got up and went to the bedroom. The pencil that had been imprisoned in his hand sent clacking across the table. Left behind was his book. A book filled with markings. Letters. Some big, some small.

Jane widened her eyes at Michael. Looked towards the window that was framed by a wire curtain rail but no curtains. Towards the glass, black and melted. Towards the wall that held a shadow to the ceiling, charred and coming away from the beams. Even in this dull light it contrasted the flickering of the candles.

Fount him in the cut. Cor juss leave him there.

The lad stood shaking. Head down.

Well what was he doin in the cut?

Ye ask him, Michael said, leaning against the door and pulling off his boots, each of them sucking from his feet and running water onto the floor. I juss fount him in there.

I reckon yow saved me life, the lad said.

So ye do ave a voice then.

Yes.

A name?

The lad looked down. Jane looked at Michael. She tilted her head and frowned. That frown coupled with a squint that said: How's that work?

Luke came holding a bundle of beige.

Cheers son.

Jane looked at the lad. Ya welcome to goo in the bedroom to get out a them wet clothes. We can dry em by the fire.

The lad thanked her and went into the bedroom clutching the towel to his chest.

Michael removed his trousers, followed by the overcoat and shirt. Luke laughed and pointed.

What?

Ya hair, Luke replied, laughing even more.

He tapped the palms of his hands over his hair. It was slick to his head aside from thin ringlets that popped up like corkscrew bushes.

That funny is it? he said. The laugh of a child that he had not heard in a long time, a laugh from deep inside the belly. Even now, in the midst of all this, he cor help but smirk.

Iss really funny, Luke said.

Jane caught his eye. Her eyes glistened and flickered about, looking him up and down, searching the landscape of his face. Her own face stern, rimmed by soft light. He knew what she was asking.

Talk about it later.

Gone?

Later.

She frowned and turned away. She looked thinner than he remembered. Day know whether that was him remembering wrongly or simply not knowing what her size really was.

Well, shall I give him ya spare long johns? she said.

Can do.

Yowm too nice sometimes, Michael Cash.

The lad came through the door with wet clothes in one hand and holding the towel around his waist with the other. Clothesless he looked even younger, perhaps not even fifteen. His skinny frame and hairless body looked like a brass fork. Jane took his wet clothes and handed him the long johns.

Back to ya studies now, Luke.

Luke sat back at the table. Michael pulled the long johns up his legs. He handed his clothes to Jane, who was at the fire folding the lad's over a mesh wire clotheshorse.

Did yow find him? she whispered.

Nay. But doe worry.

Doe worry? He could a killed us. What about the…

She whispered even quieter, almost as if her lips were moving but producing no sound. The gold?

Later, he hissed.

Luke watched them. Michael walked to the table and pulled out a chair and sat down. What ye werkin on?

Spellin.

Spellin! Can ye spell mar name?

Luke looked down and held his finger to his mouth. Shook his head.

That meks two of us, Michael said, and started laughing.

Jane stared at him. Wet shirt in hand. The lad came from the bedroom and waited in baggy long johns. She offered him a seat by the fire.

Soon the lad was dried out. They sat around whilst the evening got later and later and Cain slipped further away. Once or twice, Michael looked around the room and wondered if he had everything he needed. This lad he'd pulled from the cut could work a job and pay his way and they could forget about the gold and move on.

And then the lad started for his clothes.

What ye doin? Michael said.

Bess be off. Yowve done enough for me. The lad dropped the long black shirt over his head, still damp-looking and filthy.

Ye can stay as long as ye want.

Jane shot daggers at him. If he wants to goo, love.

Om sayin he doe ave to is all. Said he has no place to live.

I do, the lad said, pulling on his trousers. Thank ya both, but now I should go.

At least wait til the rain stops, Michael said. He was almost pleading now. Nothing was solid any more. Everything was slipping through his fingers. He could have already been after Cain, but he saw the lad. He wanted him to stay. He wanted something good to come from this.

They saw the lad off at the front door. The cold air threw itself into their faces like moths to fire. The storm had moved on and left behind a lingering mist.

Yow day really think he would stay did ya? Jane said.

No more gold in the mine, Michael said.

We doe need it. She rested her hand on his upper arm.

They watched the figure of the lad disappear into the mist.

XIII

After Luke was sent to bed, Michael sat fireside tearing up old newspapers and rolling them into flutes.

So am yow to tell me what happened then?

The flutes were placed between the firewall and the ash grate. Then his hands formed a spadelike shape and poked them in.

Yow left me an Luke to clean up that mess.

He gathered the coal bucket. There were only specks of slack that scrummed the bottom. Getting cold, need to buy more, he thought. He scraped up what was left and drizzled it around the paper.

The smoke smoothed up around the coal where the paper was heated from the smoulder before igniting in curls of blue flame.

Am yow listenin?

He reached out and held her hand and sat her down at the table.

I went to the church. The vicar said a praya for us. Then I fount it. Or it fount me. No. He any tests we. Gold's gone from the mine. That was all of it. I doe see any other way. Cain's gone but he can be fount. He… Heyull show me how, like He did before.

Jane shook her head. Yow still ay right. Yowm sick. She reached to touch Michael's forehead. He drew back.

Om gooin, he said.

Inside the bedroom he took a pair of dry trousers patched about the legs and pulled on a woollen coat. A creak. Behind him Luke stirred. Standing over the other side of the room, Michael stared into the dark.

Father?

Juss poppin out, son. Back soon.

By the front door, Jane held his arm and looked up at him with tears standing in her eyes. They looked like wet glass.

We doe need it, she said.

Course we do. No other way.

An how long will it tek yow? Ya doe know. Juss leave it. Juss come and sit down. What about the house an all? Brownhills am to turf us out.

She pulled at his arm. He held her by the cheeks. They were hot, almost steaming.

Oll find him. Doe worry. Oll bring it back. There's none left in the mine. Nothin left in there for us. Trust me. He needs school. He cor be down there like them other lads.

Yowm talkin stupid.

Know what om doin.

Then, as he reached for the door: Of bin earnin fourpence a week.

He turned to her. What?

Fixin shoes, Jane continued. To pay for his school. She wiped her tears with the back of her fingers.

He knew she was, but still he said, Since when?

Since yow ay bin able to get second work. Again she seized him by the arm. Doe goo. We doe need it. Juss get back on track with ya normal work.

It ay good enough.

Luke needs his father, not money.

He opened the door. She stepped across him, blocking his path.

He could a murdered us whilst we kipped. All three of us. Now yowm gooin after him?

Need to get it back.

Ya doe! Am yow not listenin? We doe need it.

I cor juss let it goo. Not like that. He shook his head. Not like that.

He pushed her aside and stepped out into the night.

After he had seen her working on those shoes he had pictured himself ambushing her. A fullblooded condemnation of her deceit. Now she had confessed, he had no joy. Another thing taken from him. But then he felt a wave of shame caused by the fact that he had even wanted to ambush her in the first place.

The mine was shining. All the field of mud they called the bank was sparkling white and blue. A thin layer of frost. Not even the bruised air could degrade it. It shone and fluttered. To him it was but another sign. Like the North Star. Cain had the fortune but He was any testing him. It could be fount.

He knocked on the undermanager's office door. Opened it.

A scramble for a candle. Naked skin on skin. The long red locks of a wench. Lawrence reaching for his trousers and falling on his face. Shit, she said, and pulled up her trousers. A bankswoman. Younglooking. Past him she went and out into the dark.

Oh, Michael said.

A groan. Up from behind the desk came Lawrence, his face red as a furnace.

The fuck is that?

Sorry sir, iss Michael. Cash.

What the fuck do... what time is it?

Iss late evenin. But I was comin by to ask ye somethin.

Lawrence adjusted a Davy lamp. He stood smoothing his hair down, still with his shirt unbuttoned. He spoke whilst dressing.

What an earth could be worth ye coming ere at this hour?

Need to know where Cain's lodgins am.

Lawrence shook his head. Out of the question. We cor give out anythin like that.

Michael looked out onto the bank. Cold winds whistling. The woman was moving across it like a ghostly shadow. That a bankswoman? he said. What's ya wife bound to say about that?

Lawrence stopped buttoning his shirt. A tight curl formed upon his glowing face. Maybe the light or maybe the blood in his cheeks.

Yowm a piece a werk.

Juss need the address.

Why?

Find him.

Whass ya trouble wi him?

Doe believe thass any a ya business.

Lawrence's smirk turned flat. Now shadows formed upon his brow. Think he woe be back?

Ay sure.

Listen, I cor give out information like that, Lawrence said, flattening his hair against his scalp before pulling on a coat. Iss in the top drawer. Gooin for a smoke.

Michael watched Lawrence duck his head down out the door. No later than the sound of wood in the hole, he stood over the top drawer rifling through the folders, leaving black fingerprints on them as he went. In the third folder assigned surname H, he found it. CAIN HILL. RESIDENCE: NO. 4 COLLIERSFORD, HIGH HEATH.

Outside he stepped through Lawrence's pipesmoke. Then he turned back.

Oh, an did me wife come by an ask about ouses?

Lawrence glared. His eyes sharp and vicious. It was as though he cor believe he was being asked questions like nothing had happened. Like Michael day just catch him holding skin on skin with that lass. Eventually he spoke.

She popped by the office. Explained ya situation. Doe think iss worth ye gooin lookin for Cain, for whatever reason.

Where am they?

The ouses? We've places here and there, but there's a list. Some people bin waitin longer than ye, ever thought about that?

Might miss a shift tomorra, but I reckon there's some nice lumps that will be picked in me stall.

Oh ar, Lawrence said, readjusting his pipe as it clacked against his teeth. An I suppose yowll be wantin to be paid for it.

Ye can juss give it me wife when ye sort that new place for her. No scrip an all. Cash only.

Lawrence looked at him, half in the shadows, half shining with reflected frosted land. He was leaning against the office, underneath a window that held a broken lamp above it. Ay my job, he said.

Is it ya job to be messin about wi them bankswomen?

Lawrence removed his pipe and spat into the ground. Breathed smoke into Michael's face. One shift's pay, he said, an oll put in a word to see to ya family in one of our places in the next two days. Thass it.

Michael nodded. Ar. Sounds fair.

Lawrence spat again. Thought ye was a good man.

What makes a good man?

XIV

THROUGH the village's buildings, commons and gardens a deep copper cast. Silence save the drag of wind through the trees that stretched their branches like massive broken fingers.

At least he woe have to worry about the family out in this cold. Jane day realise he did everything for them, for the boy. If she did, she woe have tried to stop him from leaving.

Towards the end of the village, across the small triangle of common, what once was grass but now a hard patch of black earth, came two foxes darting, one chasing the other. It was the nature of the fox to dwell at night, and he had become all too used to seeing and hearing them.

He stopped at the pub. A dim orange glow broken by

dark bodies. Voices murmuring in a low hum. He thought about going in, but day.

The road to High Heath split through cornfields. He balled his hands in the pockets of his coat as the wind bit at his exposed face. Every now and then the moonlight shot through the smoky sky.

He wondered whether Cain would be there or nay. He had fount Michael's address, so surely he would know Michael had fount his. Still he had to be ready. If Cain was there, sat with his feet up in front of the fire with a fistful of gold, what then? He blew into his balled fists. They felt like cold clutches of bone.

Skeletons of corn plants lined up in a lake of graves with their husks wilted and sparkling with frost. Amongst them a rustling.

He stopped and looked down. Dashes of what seemed like small rodents. The corn plants day stop scratching in the wind until he reached the end of the fields.

It was a miniature village of sorts. First, an open oss road. To the east a small stable with wire fencing. In the near distance an L-shaped block of small houses connected around a dirt courtyard where two wooden benches lived next to a tall wooden post.

The post read RIDDING'S GROVE. He looked about for any side streets. To the west across a small common was another row of small houses.

A door opened and out came a man with a little dog. It spotted Michael and went about sniffing and pawing at his leg.

Patch, shouted the man, now stood at the end of his yard. Doe mind him, he's saft.

Michael reached for the dog and felt its wet nose against his knuckles.

Am ya lost?

Lookin for Colliersford.

The man pointed to the line of houses to the west and said, See them ouses there? Juss follow them down and to the left and there it is. Seems like more an more ouses am being built, wonder if they ave enough folk to live in them.

Michael thanked the man and went on his way. The wind had calmed now and all about the air felt frozen and still. The sky a strange purple as the moon broke free of its smoky shackles. The small row of houses was lined with young trees barely three foot high. He followed them and stepped across a brook that ran next to another farmer's field. The brookwater trickled along. Perched at its bank a group of frogs with their throats bubbling and eyes bulging. Just as the man with the dog had said, along the brook, to the side of the houses, was Colliersford.

Down the thin path sat tucked away and uneven on the ground small bungalows all lit up save one, the fourth. He went down its yard and peered through the window.

Darkness. He knocked the door. Looked back again at the window. Nothing. At the end of the yard again he observed the row of lodgings. All lit up, all smoking from their chimneys. All but number four.

He could try to open the door. It might be unlocked. He day have a candle or lamp. Perhaps the moonlight would aid him. He walked to the door once more. Reached out. What if he is in there. If he is waiting in the dark. Michael's mind raced. Then he thought about Luke. About the gold. The fire. He grabbed the handle and—

Hello.

He jumped out his skin and turned to the voice. A shiny eye full of moonlight peering from a halfopened door. The neighbouring bungalow.

Am lookin for Cain. Lives here.

Why.

Ave ye sin him comin an gooin recently? Wi bags or anythin?

No. The eye was held wide open and fixed on him firm.

Another voice came from inside the house, deeper, hoarser. The door shut. It opened again, fully this time. Standing in the way was a tall man in long johns with a sootblack face. A miner.

He's gone, the miner said. Left earlier. Had a bag an all.

Michael felt a strange relief. Cain wor there. Knew he would be chased.

Did he say where he was gooin?
Said he was gooin hum.
Where he was frum, or where he was born?
No difference, the miner said.
Did he say where exactly?
The miner scratched his head. Does he owe ya money?
Somethin like that, Michael said.

XV

WHEN he reached the small village north of Walsall, he rested on a bench by the roadside. A litter of houses and stores were still sleeping under the bronze sky. He watched the clouds move. Southward a deeper burning. Calling him. Cain was going home. He had to be on the way to Dudley, or already there. The road ahead led to Walsall, on to Dudley, on to Cain.

Onward an oss and cart came past. He stepped aside the road and watched it go with the driver tipping his cap and shouting on his whinnying nag.

He followed the long road. To the east and the west lay large fields, some farmed and some wildlooking with long weedgrass frostriddled and swaying gently in the wind. And these lands dipped and curved around small ponds and brooks that seemed to swallow all light.

The gold was fount for a reason, he repeated to himself. It was taken for a reason too. It can be fount again, even if it means travelling through the cold night, and the warm industrial red night.

Across the field to the east came a small herd of deer. They stepped tentatively and bent to the ground to crunch up and get under the clumps of weed and when he stopped they each lifted their heads and stared at him. They were but dark shapes along the land. When he carried on, they halfbolted across the grass and widened their berth.

The more he walked the brighter the sky became. The land around him became more visible not by sunrise but through beams of industrial light, flickering like the flame of some massive candle. What was usually his horizon started becoming his zenith.

Ahead the structures of the town were akin to the rolling hills of the countryside, with their mounds and folds that go up and up, peaking at a church that dominated the skyline. Its spire reached up into the redness and branded it with its crucifix. Instead of trees and heather and sheep, there were brick factories and kilns bursting with fire and chimneys, some big and some small, some clustered and fat, some separated and thin. The smoke that billowed around was starker than any morning mist. This land looked as though it had been pulled up from what was once underneath: an open wound.

Shouts of men and stamps of osses. The chant of iron being worked and furnaces being fed coal.

Michael followed the wide road that led towards the town centre and stopped a man that went by on oss and cart.

Whass the bess way to get to Dudley?

The cartdriver pulled up and looked down at him. Probably the cut, he said. Barges goo there all the time, which yowm wantin to get on over yonder. The cartdriver pointed to the west. Over the ironworks bridge. Om agooin that way an all. Can tek ya.

He thanked the driver and mounted the cart. The driver whipped the leather reins.

The oss was patched white against black. He pictured it white, but it appeared more like burnt skin. A scarred oss on scarred land. It dripped with brass and leather.

Behind him in the cart lumps of ore and chain in open wooden boxes. The wheels rolled over uneven road, split by the clunking of the osses' iron shoes.

At the bank of the canal the smoke from the chimneys rolled about and drowned the air. Barges moved through it under the heat of the town in two lanes. Incoming and outgoing. They broke through the smoke as it snaked across the cut and back out the other side. Men lugged boxes of chain and other ironwork from cart to barge and barge to cart.

As the mule moved deeper into the smoke Michael held his sleeve to his mouth. It felt as though his gullet was inflating. Why's this smoke so arsh? he said, muffled.

Ay smoke, the cartdriver said, smoke rises.

What is it then?

Devil's breath. More like a fog.

Michael coughed into his sleeve. He turned to the cartdriver and said, What in God's creation sorta fog is this?

The cartdriver laughed. Whatever it is, God day create it.

They got off. Out in the yards, chains were being stamped and bent and forged and linked. Nobody seemed to mind the fog.

He watched them work by the burning skylight created by the furnaces. The cartdriver approached a banked barge. Shapes of people coming along the water's edge. That and the still, dark shadows of the workosses attached to the barges. Michael hunched over coughing into his sleeve. When he pulled his face from it, his arm was covered in oildark spit. He stared. It worried him. Thicker than any spit, darker than any shadow.

Jane day want ye to go. But she lied to ye. Watched ye work yaself sick, all the time earning money.

He unbuttoned the coat and rubbed away the sweat that beaded on his head. Beneath his feet a stew of soot and ash and mud and oss shit. The cartdriver walked back towards him.

Alright am ya?

Ar, Michael said, juss warm is all.

The cartdriver looked him up and down. Alright, he said, that uns gooin to Dudley, help me unload this cart an yowll ave a seat on it. Theym always lookin for more men on the barges.

XVI

THERE was nobody else on board save the bargeman. He stood at the front shouting the workoss along. Over the edge scarce any cutwater visible for both lines of barge pushed past one and other. The scrapes of metal on metal.

Michael was closer to the shouts of the bargeman behind them. A lad nay a day older than the one he fished from the canal. He watched the lad, stood with one leg raised at the front of his barge shouting confidently to chainmakers in the yards.

When they got clear of the foundries he stood up at the front of the barge and asked about Dudley.

Be there few hours before sunrise, the bargeman said.

He looked ahead where the sky turned back from a faint clayed glow to dark blue. Lines of workosses along the coalblack banks. Behind and ahead an unending line of barges. They passed houses with yards just off the canal. They passed under bridges where figures sat straddling the edges. Some shouting welcomes and others shouting filth.

And he wondered what might happen when he got there. Cain was willing to do anything. Even if he could be fount, there would be a fight. He day know if he could win. He started to question if it was worth it. He day expect to feel relieved to find Cain wor at home. That worried him.

Charlie, the bargeman said.

He took his eye from the landscape. Charlie the bargeman stared at him.

Michael, he said.

So whym ya gooin a the night?

Michael coughed and spat onto the bank. Why do ye ask?

Juss wonderin. Yow ay labourin there.

An ye know that for a fact?

I know every man that travels this way. Have to. It ay safe enough on the cut at night otherwise. Yowm new.

Charlie faced forwards and slowly organised the reins in between his hands.

Michael coughed again. Am lookin for someone.

Who yafter?

Nevermind.

None a me business is it? Well, I told ya I know every person that comes this way. Might ave sin ya man.

Michael cleared his throat and spat. He wiped his mouth with his sleeve. Short bloke. Loud. Name's Cain.

Charlie turned the information over in his head. Muss not ave come this way. Ow do ye know he's gooin to Dudley?

Faith, I suppose.

Nothin good ever come from chasin after someone. An I doe believe in that nonsense about lost sheep an all that. The Bible says Jesus left his flock to get back one lost sheep. Well, suppose he day find the lost un, an then he gets back an his flock am gone an all. Charlie shook his head. Nay, never did trust that book.

Ow do ye know I ave a flock to leave beyind? Michael said.

They crashed against the barge in front. The dull clang of metal against metal. Charlie instantly pulled on the reins of the workoss and shouted Whoa, whoa. A whistle. Michael lurched forward and steadied himself against the boxes. Then the lad's barge slowly shunted into theirs. Another whistle. Ahead under a fog that flowed over the iron bridge came running men in black clothing like giant alleycats. They held tools. Hammers and picks.

Not again, Charlie shouted, and took a whistle from his pocket and blew.

They crawled over the barges that were further along the cut passing off boxes to smaller shapes that seemed to be boys weaving in and out of the workosses along the bank and under the bridge. All along the cut now whistles blew from every boat.

The bargeman jumped from his stand and searched down the side of the cargo. He pulled up a red toolbox. Fuckin cunts, he said as he unlatched the box and went inside. Not mar barge. Then he looked up to Michael. Stay ere, he said. From the box he pulled a pistol. He stood looking it up and down for a moment. Checking its readiness. Meanwhile the robbers advanced with their wanton war cries, bellowing like some great phantom steam engines. Michael was frozen. The shouting of the workers and robbers. The faint ink of the bridge. The slosh of the cutwater. The whinnying and frightened kicks of the workosses. They all pulsed in his ears. As the ghostly figures of the robbers became more visible he felt some movement about his thigh and saw that his hands were shaking.

By now three robbers were on the barge in front. Two threw wild punches and kicks at the bargeman whilst one lifted the boxes. Charlie scrambled to the front of the barge, levelled the pistol and fired.

A momentary quiet came over the cut. The robbers scrambled away each of them from one barge to the next until they reached the bridge. Michael found his way over the boxes and alongside Charlie. A few barges down, a man was being wrestled to the ground by three bargemen. On the boat in front lay a body.

They vanished as quickly as they came. All that remained was the captured robber, now tied up and slumped over a workoss who kicked and shouted in protest, and the body. Charlie turned the latter over and swiftly pulled off its mask. The body of a child. The bargemen and loaders were stood around holding lamps above their heads. Some sighed. Some turned away. One shouted, For God's sake.

Why the bloody hell did ya shoot him? a loader said.

Charlie still held the pistol by his side, looking down at the body. It looked nothing much. A pool ringed around its head. It was pale grey, and the soft brown hair fluttered in the wind. Michael held his hand flat on the crown of his head. He day stop looking at the body for a while. All the sounds around him were smothered. How easy a life was taken in this ransacked land.

The bargeman in front was leaning up against the side of his barge. He was old and had black blood running from his temple. A few men tended to him. One held up a balled shirt against the wound.

We should get him back, a worker shouted.

Om fine, the hurt man said.

Yowm gooin pale, another said. Bess to be safe.

They fetched the hurt man to his feet and took him over the other side of the cut into a barge for Walsall. A loader took up the reins to drive his barge. The remaining men stood about still looking at the body.

What should we do with him?

Take him on to Dudley, sort it then.

An the one thass livin?

Him an all.

Someone cover the poor lad up.

Of lost six boxes of iron.

Yowm worryin about that?

Thass money om losin. We work honestly and this un chose to steal. I say he got what he deserved.

Ay nobody deserves that.

They all went, each to his own barge. Returning to work and slowly the stream of barges started up again.

Charlie was sat still holding the pistol. He looked up with eyes glazed over like a whetstone. Had to do it, he said. No choice. No choice. They wor gettin mar barge. Not marn. Why am lads so saft? Whass he doin on the rob? Lord, forgive me.

Michael knelt and reached for the weapon. Let me take it, he said.

The man sat before him was stiff as a board and pale as a sheet. No. Oll tell them there was no choice.

Who?

Them. The police. Everyone.

Thass fine. Juss give me the gun. Doe want ye doin anything silly with it.

Charlie's voice was hoarse and unsteady. Michael could see now that he wor very old himself. A younger man than he.

Do ye think I meant it for a lad?

Course not. Juss let me ave this, he said, gently prying the pistol out of stiff hands.

The barges in front had been clear for a bit. Michael could see the black cutwater rolling under the moonlight. He pocketed the pistol, grabbed the reins of the workoss, and shouted it on.

Perchance he should not have come. Perchance Cain ay even in Dudley. He pictured his family tucked up in bed, fast asleep whilst the cold bit at his face. The boy lying dead on the barge ahead out in all that cold and all that dark wor much older than his own. Where be his father?

And then he was met by the truth in that he himself wor with his son. He wor there to watch over him. Perhaps, if he day come back soon, someone would see Luke and ask themselves the same question: Where be his father?

He sighed and watched pale rags of breath shoot from his mouth. Felt the weight of the pistol swell in his pocket.

XVII

At Dudley the barge came to a stop in the unloading dock. A large crowd of people were huddled canalside. He stepped off the barge. Charlie was still sat with his head down.

The crowd was in front of the dead boy, who was laid out on a pallet of wood, powderwhite save his blackened midriff. People were chattering to one and other, and the men that Michael pushed past scowled.

Was yow that killed the boy? one said.

Nay, Michael said, turning back to the barge. Wor him either.

A uniformed officer came from the crowd. He went over to the barge, trailed by some few nosy stragglers. He started to lift the bargeman up and out onto land.

But Michael wor thinking about that. Not about Charlie or the slain lad, but Cain. And he was finally here. Where Cain could be. Where he's frum. An if he's here an the gold an all then oll do anythin.

He asked a passerby where the nearest pawner was.

In town. Other side a the castle.

He said his thanks and followed the path through the works.

Steady streams of loaders and unloaders took carts of lime from waggons to the outgoing barges. They unloaded the incoming barges of their coal and iron and threw them on other mule-led waggons. Yards were filled with chain and their links the size of loaves of bread around and thick as black pudding.

And in these yards fire and hearth roared from the furnaces. Coal melted iron. Land burned land. Men carried chain and worked it with tongs and hammer, bending it to their will.

Ahead the giant chimneys stabbed the near landscape like some massive nails driven into the palms of the land. And the land seeping coal black as day.

Further south atop a hill sat the castle. Mostly destroyed and derelict. Its stone foundations reaching up from the blackness like the carcass of some giant prehistoric mammal. Trees sideclung. To the west giant brick kilns bloomed from the earth like permanent weeds.

And from them limesmoke. All this a picture of what looked to him like nothing he had ever seen before. A land eating itself like a dog chewing its leg off to escape a snare.

Suddenly it came to him that he could be too late. Time had passed. The gold could be pawned and the money spent or lost. Who knew. Still, he had to try and find Cain.

He reached the end of the path that led to a road around the castle. The clamour of the works was felt down the back of his neck. He looked up and from the floating smoke dark drops of rain started to fall softly onto his face.

Downhill from the castle the town was hardly visible under a dark plumage. He followed the oss road. People driving carts passed him. He lifted his head and said good morning to each of them. They responded with greetings of one kind or another. Nods. Waves. Hellos. Questions without answers. Ow bist yow.

Michael down the town's high street, where the earliest openers unlocked their doors. He wondered whether the sun had risen yet. With eyesight alone there was no way of telling.

He went into the first shop he saw, a butcher's, who pointed him in the direction of Tim Smith, a local dealer in metalware.

The shop was full of glass cabinets and wooden shelving. There were some wooden shields with thin metal stamps on their fronts, glass ornaments in the cabinets, silver signets and chain necklaces and bracelets.

The front desk had a round bell on it. He tapped it three times. Waited. Shuffling steps on stone. A head came from under the desk. Michael peered over the top at the man coming from the cellar.

Ow bist!

Tim Smith?

Call me Smithy, the man said, turning around and dropping the cellar door. He was wheezing. He had a black eye and swollen lip. What can I do ye for?

I was told ye was a pawner?

Om a dealer, he said, not a pawner. Buy an sell.

Whass the difference?

Pawners borrow people money in exchange for what they own. If they doe pay back, they lose what they pawn. Nay. Would never be a pawner. Too much trouble that is.

Smithy was wiping the sweat from his brow with a pale yellow cloth. He was a fat man. Michael could still hear his wheeze.

Do ye know the nearest one?

There ay any pawners ere.

Oh.

Ar. Probably for the same reason. Iss daft business that is. Anyroad, buyin or sellin?

Neither. Lookin for someone. I reckon they might ave bin to this place. An they was carryin somethin valuable.

Somethin they were after sellin?

Ar.

Well. This past wik's bin quite busy. Whole lot comin in an out. Bought a few expensive things. Signets, chains, a brooch. Was ye after an old lady with a brooch?

Nay, he said, scratching his head. This would a bin yesterdy.

Smithy set down his handkerchief and rested his hands on his sides. His wheezing stopped. Well. If ye tell me what ya man was sellin…

Man called Cain. Quite short. Probably filthylookin. A miner.

Lots a miners round ere. What was he sellin?

Michael stared at him. A pause.

Doe wanna tell? Smithy said. Well, I cor elp ya then.

Gold.

Rings? Chains? What?

Juss rough gold.

Smithy's eyes widened. I know who yowm referrin to. The metalware specialist. Thought I was lyin he did. Told him to fuck off.

What ye mean?

Well, he wor happy with me valuation, was he? As some tend to be. Then he says he was bein cheated an wanted to know where the mine owners lived, ye know, the well-off folk. So he could goo an cheat them instead.

Cheat them?

Get more than iss wuff.

Cain's greed ay surprising, he thought.

And?

Cor tell him if I wanted to. Mad if he thinks theyull buy it off him juss like that.

What did ye tell him then?

Smithy sat down onto the wooden stool behind the desk and let out a deep sigh.

Pointed him in the direction of the limestone pits. Said the manager there would know the owner's addresses.

Thank ye, Michael said, turning to leave.

Not sure iss werth chasin him, by the way. Of sin blokes like him before. Dangerous types.

Oll be alright.

He went back up the hill that led to the castle ruins. Down at the works he noticed hardly a thing. No person or oss, no barge or cart. Everything looked as if it was burning alive.

On the other side of the hill the kilns shed bright white clouds, lifting into the sky. Through the haze was the cut that split through the middle, the cut he came in along.

Dustsplashed osses pulled carts filled with coal and waggons carried stone towards the kilns. Around the edge of the scene caverns lifted and burst through the surface. Workers filed in and out under the arches that lead into the land. They looked like giant melted circles. Smooth and pulled apart like hot glass.

At the opening of the pits people moved in and out freely. Their skin dusty and drier than sunbleached bone. The light that went through the opening reached only partway into the cavern. From then on darkness. The workers disappeared with it. At the same time others came ghostlike from the dark, shielding their eyes and pushing carts of stone. If Cain was mixing in with this crowd, he would be easy to spot. A black sheep.

A woman with dry skin like overused coal. Michael asked for the manager and she looked at him and pointed into the tunnel she came from. Blackness save dusty outlines of bodies like some otherworld apparitions.

Inside: torchlit men, women and children crawling over each other. They picked at the walls and carried pieces of stone in groups, some pieces larger than a man, and pushed carts and kicked the dust around the pit and coughed and shouted to one and other.

He could find Cain and take the gold back. But he wor at home and he wor around the pawners and he wor here neither. Was Jane right? Was it worth it? Luke needs a father, but his future needs the gold. But how long would he be gone in search of it?

He felt the dust move in and around his throat and bent over coughing, holding his arm to his mouth. He coughed and coughed, and nobody stopped to help. Day have time. They worked. They were coughing an all. The chalkwhite pit was shining in the torchlight and shaking under the picks and chisels.

Michael lifted himself up again. Still he held his sleeve to his mouth and breathed like rakes on gravel. The undermanager is always easy to spot. He is the man shouting loudest. Michael went up behind him and tapped him on the shoulder.

Yes, yes, what ye want? the undermanager said.

Was told ye met a man called Cain who was after the owner's address.

What?

Past them came two young boys pushing a small cart. The undermanager took his whip and let it go over their backs. As he cocked his arm back a third time, Michael grabbed it. The undermanager turned his head viciously.

A man called Cain, Michael shouted. Came to ye after sellin gold to the owner of this pit.

Let goo.

Michael loosed the arm. For a moment it seemed as though the undermanager would throw him out. Then he sighed and said, Yes. Came an went.

Where?

He looked at Michael and frowned. Am ye police? Doe look it.

No. Juss—

Well, what ye after him for?

Michael watched the undermanager coiling the leather whip around his fist. It seemed like something he did out of habit. Weem partners, Michael said, looking around the pit. Thass all. Juss tryin to catch up with him.

Right, well we ay supposed to give out the owners' residence, but iss mostly common knowledge anyroad. Told him the owners live over Tipton way. The Brierly family. A big estate. Cor miss it.

Thank ye, Michael said, coughing into his sleeve.

Oll tell ye like I told him. It woe werk. Them families want nothin to do with people like us. If yowm both smart yowll stay away.

Thanks, but om gooin, he said. And he was. He had come this far. His fear of what Cain might do was still in his mind and that day stop him. Some family he had never heard of certainly wor stopping him.

From the far side of the pit a deep tumbling. Followed by a scream. They both turned to the noise. Already a small crowd was gathered. Another scream. The manager ran over. Michael followed him. Get them out! Get them out! someone shouted.

I cor, iss stuck!

Help!

The manager pushed through and Michael followed. A woman was crying and shouting. Against the pit wall a young girl lay under pieces of rock. Her upper body was free but her legs were covered. She was still and her eyes were closed. A woman knelt at her side.

Alive? the manager said.

The woman nodded.

Get these stones off.

They tried to lift the rocks one at a time. Some were watching and muttering to each other.

Already tried it.

Iss stuck.

I know what would be better for the girl.

Poor girl.

Where's the parents? Michael said.

The manager turned around. Ay got none. Ye get on ya way now.

What ye mean, none? Ow's she in ere?

Lift it, goo on, lift it, the workers groaned and shouted

at each other. They moved one piece of stone and started on the next.

On ya way, the manager said.

Michael looked around. There were more women, girls and boys than he had ever seen in a pit before. Ow's it ye all got ere? he said.

They were grouped together, eyeing him as they spoke to one another. It seemed to him they were arguing a decision. They kept staring. One looked as though she wanted to speak to him but the manager stepped towards him and scowled.

None a ya business, he said. Yowm in my pit. Get the fuck out.

Michael stared at him for a moment. This bastard was even worse than the undermanager in his pit. But it wor his pit after all. He nodded. Fine. Made for the exit.

He was stopped at the tunnel. It was a young woman. She looked at him in the halfdark, her eyes frightened and shining. He stared back at her.

They get the little uns from homes, she whispered. After theym given up as babies or their parents am dead. Keep us women in a shared ouse with them. Make us look after them. Part a the job, they say.

Michael looked at the woman, then over her shoulder. The crowd was weeping and moaning. He looked back at the woman. She got closer and grabbed him by the coat. She threw her eyes all about him madly.

Am yow truly police or what?

No, Michael said.

Her eyes became more desperate as if she thought he was lying. Help us, she said.

Om sorry. Om juss a miner.

She steadied and looked down at where her hands gripped his coat. Swanwhite knuckles borne up. Loosed hold of him. Sorry, she said.

The crowd outside the caverns stood around for over an hour before it started to disperse. It gathered to watch as a heavyset woman tried to breathe air into the girl.

Michael was on a brick wall by the cut. Since he'd sat down, he had the woman's voice in his mind. Her words. Her desperate eyes. In his mind the image of the dead boy on the narrowboat with the curl of blood around his head. The boy in the canal. The girl crushed under limestone in the pit. The nippers in the coal mine searching for scraps of candle.

Luke in his dreams, in the pits, being taken by the water. Luke with the gold, in a good school, in nice clothes. The picture of Luke as an adult man, as a farmer, or shop owner, or gentleman. Perhaps there is a son, his grandchild. Luke's son going to school and being well off.

Luke without school, without a father, driving a narrowboat. Luke stealing iron ore. Luke shot to death. Luke in these limestone caverns, crushed under stone.

It was clear to him now. He wor killing himself chasing a ghost.

XVIII

THE further he had travelled into his hunt the more he had found every road led to the same thing. He remembered the Bible instructs sobermindedness, for the enemy prowls like a lion, seeking to devour anyone who walks its path. But he was tired. He had lost the ability to be soberminded. He was so, so tired.

An if ye goo on, ye may not find it, he thought. An if ye goo back, yowm back to where ye started. An if Luke's in the mines, then—

He had to let the gold go and with it his vision for the boy's bright future, that cruel vision sent by Him and labelled a test pretending to be a vision of salvation when it was a vision of fancy, yet also gone was the crueller and more hellish vision for the boy's dark future, that future where his father was killed in pursuit of blind faith, but even then he could not escape the feeling deep in the pit of his stomach that he had failed, that real life, no visions, no fantasies, no nightmares, just pure, cold life still wor good enough, and what would the boy's future look like in this middle ground, this neither heaven nor hell offered by gold or death, it was back to before, it was life before he found gold in a coal mine, and all that came of it was torment, not by the loss of the gold but by the idea that it would ever be found again, and now it was back to hard work, back to the days of pleading, back to the pit.

So he took himself canalside and waited whilst the barges were unloaded. He took the time to sit on the filthy ground and remove his boots. He winced as his forefinger and thumb, black as tongs, pinched lightly against the blisters and cuts that painted his soles.

When he was young, he and his father would go fishing at the lake. Only when his father was not blind drunk. It was something he had never wished to do but saw its benefits when he became a man. Of all the bad his father had done, teaching him to fish had been the exception.

They waded through the shallows with wooden rods. The week before, his boots had been stolen. He had gone to swim in the lake with some other lads and left them on the grass. When his father found out, he was made to go barefoot until they could afford new ones. This included the fishing trip.

There he stumbled, his toes slipping on the rock bed underfoot. When he caught a fish, he slipped and sliced the base of his heel on what must have been glass. He pulled a sharp breath through his teeth. The grey water bloomed dark roses.

He sat inspecting it on the pebble shore. Watched the ooze of his blood along the pale pruned white of his foot. At the same time, the fish he had caught still thrashed in the water, on the end of his rod. His father grabbed it and unhooked it and slid it into his bag.

It hurts, Michael said.

His father was wrangling the rod line. After a moment he waded ashore and dropped it onto the grass. Looked down at him, at the bleeding foot.

Mercia gives and teks, he said. Pick up ya rod.

That was his father's reasoning for everything. This land, which he always took to calling by its ancient name, Mercia, through his fascination with kings he knew next to nothing about, gives and takes. All of life's fates explained by this one simple rule. There is no give without take, and Mercia's take was always fair.

◆

Michael slipped his boots back on. Dreaded the thought of getting up. Wondered whether he actually could get up. Wondered if his father was right. This land gives and teks, so does He, almost as if theym one. An if that even is true, then where in His or Its name is mine. What has it given.

Michael aboard a narrowboat. He had agreed with the bargeman to help unload in exchange for a lift back home.

As they started moving, he took one last look back at the town. Boats like giant caskets. Chainmakers in the yards. Miners in grouped locomotion. Well-dressed people midstride. Some towards the town, some away from it. Faces shielded by creamy white handkerchiefs.

They passed the big brick kilns. Limestone. When burnt it turned to quicklime. It was shovelled out the drawholes at the bottom of the kilns. Then carried in tubs across to the barges waiting canalside. It looked like hills of powder. Made to be taken to the iron foundries, to farms, even to other limestone quarries and mixed with water to build kilns that would then create more quicklime.

Thass what she died for, he said aloud. Nobody was listening.

The driver stood at the rear end, only his upper body visible above the hills of grey powder. He held a long stick and slowly plunged it into the canal. Michael realised it wor pulled by a workoss.

There was one other man at the front of the barge. He eyed Michael scornfully, as though they had met before and he had been wronged by him.

He was doing the right thing. Had to swallow his pride. At least he had been spared all his life from the lands he'd travelled through to get here. And there was nowhere worse than this place. He doubted he would ever come back again.

All the narrowboats were piloted the same way, a man pushing from the back end towards a wall of brick and land punched out by a relatively small black hole. A tunnel. The men at the front of the barges lay down on stacked pallets, some facing one way, some the other, with their legs dangling over the edge of the barge. Then they reached out their legs to meet the tunnel walls.

They started using their legs to move the barges through the tunnel. Michael realised that was his job. The scornful man must have followed his gaze, because he moved to the front of the boat and said, Called leggin. Gorra leg it through the tunnel until weem out the other side.

Is it hard gooin? Michael realised his legs were numb. He wor sure whether they had the strength to do it.

Tay too bad once ye get a stride gooin. The scornful man seemed surprisingly alright.

They lay down on the pallet at the toe of the barge. Above, the already dark day slipped into pitch black as they entered the tunnel.

Now, the scornful man said, just reach ya legs out and push. Walk like a crab does.

A crab? Michael said.

Like yowm draggin a carpet. Place ya left and drag, right and drag.

The feeling seeped back into his legs again, and with it his muscles tight as a drum painfully throbbing with each step. Boots on brick echoed throughout the tunnel. The stench of damp. Left, right, left right, the scornful man chanted.

The momentum of the boat took the strain off his legs once again. As they had done throughout his entire journey, as they seemed to have been doing for the past however many years, they moved like clockwork. Once he got them oiled and wound up, they would move. It was the starting and stopping that cursed him.

He day know how long he would have to drift through these dank veins. The soothing slap of water sent him into a lull. He realised his eyes were closed. He was still a young man, yet his body felt middle-aged. He day like how exhausted he felt. It was no way of living.

Had to swallow his pride. This shameful thought kept visiting him. Swallow ya pride, bury it deep, he told himself with each step along the tunnel walls, with each wave of water rocking against the hull of the barge. Luke's school wor his burden alone. He had to realise that now. Gold, riches. They were fanciful things. Dreamful things. Like the smooth wooden music box he once saw as a child, in the arms of the girl who lived down the road. Still he was fearful. He had already worked himself sick. Put everything into this. Now he was going back.

He opened his eyes. The blood vessels stung as they drowned in the daylight. The barge was coming to the end of the tunnel. He closed and opened them until they stopped hurting. They legged their last along the cave walls and let the boat drift out slowly. The pilot had stepped off the rear end and was chatting to the men that affixed the chains to the carriage. Michael got up slowly and turned himself round. The scornful man was sat upright with his feet resting atop the water. It looked almost as if he was standing on it.

They got going again. Another link in the incessant train of waterriders. The weight of the pistol still sagged his trousers. He wanted to be rid of it. It was a bitter taste in his mouth. The reminder of what he was willing to do. He looked over the side and into the black cutwater. Reached into his pocket. As he did, he looked up. They were passing a wide field of mud at the outside of some works that were in turn surrounded by pockets of pine groves. Out stepped from the nearest grove a figure. A man. Unmistakable. Towards the cut came Cain.

XIX

HE saw Cain and nothing but Cain. Everything else disappeared. The realisation that had made him board a boat home included. It was only Cain and the gold now. God any tested him.

Here it is. He brung it to ye. Goo after it. Ay chasin a ghost now. Iss right there. Iss Luke's future. Iss werth the risk.

Michael leaped from the barge and started after the thief. Someone shouted after him but he day hear. He went across the black earth as quickly as his legs would let him. Cain slowed his walk to a stroll after he locked eyes on Michael. Then stopped.

Yowm alive, Cain said. He turned his head to the side and spat. Showed his crooked brown smile.

Michael had not forgotten it. As if he had seen it a

thousand times before. In the face of his father. In the face of countless old undermanagers with their whips. Where is it? he said.

Where's what?

The gold ye nicked frum me. Michael reached into his pocket and felt cold iron at his fingertips.

Gold? What gold? Cain said, looking behind him to the trail. It led through small bunches of dead bushes and disappeared into the grove.

Why tek it? Ye knew ow much I need it. I told ye. That gold's everythin to me. To me family. Ye knew that an ye still did it. Me boy cor—

Yes, yes, yes. Ye boy needs school! Ye want to be a good man. Trouble is, sometimes ye cor be a good man an ave what ye want at the same time. Of fount it works much better to be the other sort a man. If ye want somethin, ye ave to tek it.

Michael pulled the pistol from his pocket. Like this? he said.

Cain's face relaxed and showed white lines across his sootpainted forehead. He smiled. Somethin like that, ar.

Even now Michael was still fearful of him. He kept the pistol high and stepped forwards. He stopped about six feet away. Chuck it, he said, an thass the end of it.

Cain reached into his inside coat pocket. Ye woe kill me, will ye?

Not if ye give back whass mine.

Cain pulled the bundle from his coat and held it in a flat palm. Lucky I still ave it, he said.

Chuck it.

No.

What?

I woe chuck it. If ye want somethin, tek it. Ye ave yown beliefs an I ave mine.

Michael took another step closer. He held the pistol firm. Took another step. Cain's eyes fixed on him. Another step. Michael day look away from those eyes. Step. The bag was close enough now. Step. Only a few inches held between the barrel of the gun and those deep black eyes. For an instant, half a second, Michael looked towards the bundle. A slap. The gun sent across the air. The bundle pulled away. A thud against his head. Michael sent reeling.

Cain grasped for the pistol. Michael jumped on him. The pistol fell again. Michael fixed his arm around the bastard's neck. They scrapped on the grass, pulling and gouging and digging elbows into each other. Michael rolled Cain over the opposite way and lurched backwards for the pistol. He grabbed it and whirled and levelled it. Cain was running into the grove. Michael scrambled to his feet.

Inside the grove Cain snaked in between the trees. The bastard was heading down a slope and towards the road. Michael caught a clear line of sight by mounting the slope. His prey was about twenty feet away. He aimed the pistol low and fired. Perched pigeons thrown up flapping. The body fell like a sack of spuds. The crack of the pistol split through the cold air and his ears tolled a high painful clanging.

The bullet had caught Cain across the calf. He held his leg with one hand and clawed at the dirt with the other, all the while growling like some cornered beast. A look of fear poured into his eyes as he looked up at Michael, gasping for breath. Please! No! he said.

Chuck it, Michael said, his words sending stringed blood from his teeth.

Cain threw the bundle. Even though he was unsure whether it was still loaded, Michael kept the pistol on him as he toed across and squatted down slowly. The torn muscles along his back and legs were pulsing with pain. He coughed and sent blackness out and down his chin and struggled to breathe.

There. Now let me goo, Cain said, hunching over.

Ye knew we needed it. I told ye. Tay even for me, iss for me boy.

Michael cocked the hammer and stepped forwards. He had never felt so angry.

An I did the same, Cain pleaded. My son needs it. I did it for mine. Why do ye think om back ere? Juss let me goo. I need to get back to me boy. Please. Yowve beaten me. Yowll never see me again. Honest. Please!

Michael felt the bundle in his hand. The weight was slight, the clinks of the precious metal quiet. Massive pines bent over them, creaking. The racket of the works carried by wind through the grove. He looked down at Cain shaking and sobbing. His eyes like coat buttons.

Surely he was lying about his son, but it day stop Michael from feeling some horrible sickness rise in his throat when he looked upon the thing he had shot, moaning and blarting now, with deep red blood pulsing over its leg. Mercia. It gives an teks.

XX

MICHAEL dropped the pistol over the side of the barge. He was bound for home. Came upon his transport after walking a few miles. Was only then he felt safe enough to board another boat. V's of geese overhead. Michael sat low in the rear of the boat away from prying eyes. He unwrapped the bundle of cloth and fished out a piece of the precious metal. It looked duller than he remembered. He put the bundle into his coat pocket and squeezed his body in tight. The low winter sun was wide and pale. It caressed his face. He closed his eyes and slept.

He was woken to unload the barge. Blackness all around. In the distance a few etchings of trees. Further down the cut he noticed an iron bridge with a fingerpost alongside it. He asked the bargeman how far they were from his home.

Two more stops.

His back stabbed as he lifted the boxes of coal from the cut and onto the lone cart. The driver stood watching him. Michael wanted to say something. To ask him what the fuck he was looking at. But instead he pressed his hand against the lump inside his pocket. Almost there. They finished loading the cart and got back into the barge and on their way.

He sat halfdozing, watching the land drift past. To think he almost left the gold. At the time he cor have thought a worser thing than Luke being fatherless and what might have happened to him out there in the wild. He could have been almost home by now probably. But then he had seen Cain and felt the pull of the gold again. It was a test.

He took a scrap from his pocket and viewed it once more, turning it over in his hands. And what he had seen and done to get it. It would all be worth it to see their faces.

Michael stepped off the barge and onto dry land for the last time. He went through a naked wood where tree limbs and branches scratched against each other. The barked floor, hard and frostplagued, crunched underfoot.

The soft wisps of something falling. He stopped and looked up. Lazily fell the first few flakes of snow. He let it collect in his palms and rubbed his hands together and ran them over his face. By the time he left the wood onto the Nest Common that surrounded the canal, thin snow shirted the land.

Aside the cut bloodred berries carried tiny white lumps of snow and waterfowl slapped about the frozen reedwater. Birds were everywhere. Robins, starlings, sparrows and ringnecked doves. He had missed them. He took a deep breath and felt the crisp, fresh air fill his throat.

Lawrence sat reading a newspaper. He craned his neck around and frowned. Well, if it ay the biggest pain in me arse.

Juss wonderin whether ye sorted that place out for us is all, Michael said.

Lawrence folded the paper and slapped it on the desk. Took his feet down and readjusted his chair. Ar, he said, sorting through some papers. He handed one across to Michael. Have this un. Says yowm to be moved out if sacked or anythin.

Michael took the paper without looking and pocketed it. Where is it? he said.

Well, juss so appens there was availability in Colliersford.

Cain's place?

In good nick an all that. Got someone to check it an move ya family in this morn.

Thanks a lot, Lawrence.

Lawrence nodded and opened a drawer and fetched out a money bag and from it he took a stack of coins. Ya pay for today, as agreed, he said.

Michael shook his head. Iss alright. Yowve done enough for me. I appreciate it.

The colliery manager frowned. Sure?

Ar.

Lawrence replaced the coins and folded the bag over with his thumbs and dropped it into the drawer. So, did ye find what ye was after?

Somethin like that.

The fields were being cleared. One side was already stripped for compost. The corn skeletons taken and the ground made ready for the new season and with it the new life.

Young lads ran around with sticks, messing about in the hedgerows. They laughed and shouted to one another before running over to the track. There was a sheepdog following them that sniffed at his trousers. One of the lads started walking alongside Michael and looked up at him with a beady bird's eye. Whym ya so filthy? he said.

Om a miner.

Coal miner?

Ar.

Me grandfather was a miner. He's dead now.

One of the other lads shook a stick at the dog and threw it along the track. The dog went off like a bullet.

Michael nodded to the men working the field and said, Ya father over there?

Yes. Weem farmers. All these fields am ours.

One of the working men shouted the lads over and they went off without saying goodbye. He day mind. He was heading to his new home, to his own boy.

Jane was talking to the neighbour over the wall when he arrived. He unlatched the gate and went in and shut it behind him. The two women stared.

Alright, he said.

Jane's look of surprise relaxed and her eyes turned cold. Me husband, Michael, she said to the neighbour.

Betty. Nice to meet yow.

Michael still stood by the gate, hands in coat pockets. We met lass night, believe it or not.

Betty raised her eyebrows and let out a nervous sigh. Oh really. Ya look different in the daytime. I suppose it meks sense now why ya came over lass night. I tell ya this, itull be lovely to have another family next door. That bloke was a strange un. Up all hours rantin an ravin. Tried to fight my John on several occasions.

Doe need to worry about him any more, Michael said, standing next to Jane.

Well, it was nice meetin ya both anyroad. Let ya gerron wi it.

XXI

INSIDE was spacious. More room than they had before. There was a sitting area by the fire with more than one chair, a large kitchen with scullery fire and a table. Jane had already made the place feel homely. Fire going nice and tall. Lamps stationed on the windowsills. Chairs with knitted blankets folded over them. She walked over the far side of the room to the kitchen.

So, this is the new place, he said. Lovely, ayit?

No reply. Jane instead went about cleaning the shelves and tabletops.

Luke?

Still no reply.

Jane.

Silence.

He took the bundle from his coat pocket, walked over, and dropped it onto the table.

Jane stopped and looked at it. She carefully pulled it apart with her silent fingers and spread the cloth flat. She looked up at him. Yow left us, she said.

An now om back.

Day know when or if yow were to be back.

Om sorry.

Did yow hurt him?

Ar.

She took a deep breath and wiped her hands on her apron. Good, she said.

Luke?

At school of course.

Right, he said. Showin me the rest a the place?

Wait til yow see this, she said, leading him through a door that opened into a little hall with another two doors inside. She opened one and they went in.

This is our room, she said.

It was nothing much. A bed, a chest, a window. A little table for a light.

She took him into the other room, where a small metal cot was in the corner. Still need to get a mattress for it, she said, but he can mek do without for a few days.

Michael looked at the room. It was nothing and everything. Yet he wor able to stop himself wondering what Cain had used this room for. He lived alone, or so Michael thought he did. When then would have been the last time this room was occupied by a nipper.

Back in the main room Michael skirted the perimeter looking at details. A rainswollen panel of wood. A gathering of green mould. The dull noise the floorboards made under his heels proved shallower than his old dwelling.

In the far corner tucked away lay a small wooden chest.

Left by him, Jane said.

Michael sighed as he knelt to open it. It was beautiful wood. A rich reddish colour. He knew not what kind of wood it was but only that it was strong and heavylooking. There came a strong scent of age from it an all. He opened it. Inside was nothing. He closed the box and wondered what might have been inside before. Before the gold and before the exodus. Cain cor take a box with him but its contents must be in his bag. A photo. Money. More gold. Perhaps a locket. Does Cain have a wife somewhere else. All these questions without answers that came to him now, about Cain's life and family, real or make-believe, felt painful and piercing. They sat burrowed under the soil of his skull like slowworms.

Michael stood looking out the window. It was foggy, almost stained glass. Across it wooden bars formed a cross that separated the panes. The wind whirled flurries of snow amongst young pine trees. He held his hands to the bars and wondered if he might get used to this place, might find joy in this place, might die in this place.

They sat by the fireside. He told all. About what he had seen on the cut. About what he had seen in Dudley. About what he had done there an all. She took it all in. He apologised for how he had left, and how mad he had gone. Jane sat with legs crossed, staring into the fire.

Of let this whole thing get past me. Me head was all over the place. Sin everythin as my burden alone when I shant of. Yowve raised Luke up until now, iss any fair ye wanted to bring in some money. Juss wish yowd ave told me is all.

She scowled. An what would yowve said? Would a stopped it right there. Nipped it in the bud.

He paused in thought. There was no sound save the quiet spit of the fire. He saw Cain with the poker in hand stoking spent coals. The rug afore the fireplace was dulled with stains. Could be spilt ale from when he had fell asleep drunk on the chair Jane sat upon. Michael took a deep breath. Perhaps, he said.

I know it.

Doe matter now anyway, we ave that. He nodded towards the table.

I still want to pay me way.

Doe need to now. That should sort everythin. Michael heaved a low and rumbling cough that went on as though it was a steady drum beating. Jane offered him a handkerchief and noticed the blood dripping down the back of his hand.

That gold will kill you, she said with a tone of authority, as though she had seen it with her own eyes in some mortal vision. She stayed watching him and he could feel it. Really, she meant his pride would kill him. He knew that an all. He wiped his mouth and cleared the mess off his hand. Looked at her. Her eyes worried like those of the woman in the limestone pit.

How do yow expect to help ya son when yow cor even help yaself? she said.

Gooin to the pawner. See ow much we can get for it.

XXII

An old man behind a desk. He sat over some jewellery with an eyeglass. Michael approached him and dropped the bundle on the tabletop. The pawner's attention stayed on the stone in his hand. It was red, possibly a garnet. Michael had seen the vicar wearing red stones called garnets before. Really ought to go back there to thank him for his prayer. He cleared his throat.

The pawner took his face away from the eyeglass and stone, licked his lips, stared for a moment, and then looked down at the bundle. He dropped the stone and glass into his front shirt pocket and pulled the bundle closer.

Michael watched him undo the tie at the top and slowly reveal the gold. Some of it still locked in rock.

Some chipped clear away, shining and beautiful. The most beautiful thing he had ever seen.

The pawner clawed his eyeglass back out his pocket and lifted up a small piece of the treasure. He was making little noises as he viewed it. Hums and grunts. He put down the piece and picked up another. This one belonged to a piece of rock. It ran through the middle in a wide snaking vein. Again the pawner grunted and hummed. This he did constantly.

Michael frowned. By the time he replaced the eyeglass in his pocket he had inspected every little piece of shrapnel of what Michael had poisoned his body for, what he had witnessed murder for, what he had beaten and shot for, what he had severed the last threads of his marriage for.

The pawner looked up at him and shook his head. This ay gold.

What ye on about?

Pyrite. Fool's gold. Never heard of it?

No, no, no, Michael said, tapping his finger on the desk. Thass gold. Thass real gold mined by meself.

The pawner took a solid shining piece of the metal and held it up between his forefingers and thumbs as if it was a tiny pair of binoculars.

See ow angular an sharp it is?

An what? Iss rough. Straight frum the rock.

Wait here.

Michael nodded.

The pawner went to the back of the shop behind a screen. He returned with a small fleck of magnificent golden metal. A shining smooth pea-like pebble. This is gold, he said, see the difference?

Nonsense, Michael said, fetching up the bundle. Ay gorra clue what yowm on about.

Outside the wind felt colder and the air harsher on his lungs. The people he passed eyed him more scornfully than before. He felt as though something was afoot and that the land had turned even more sour after that conversation with the pawner. Why was the pawner trying to cheat him and why had the weather started to spite him and the people an all. He thought about going back to Jane.

No, he said aloud, there's other pawners, an all a them cor be cheats.

He stopped outside the shop and took a moment to view himself in the window. His skin was sooted, a permanent dyeing from the land, but at least he was in better shape than when he was there last. He wet his fingers with his tongue and sent them over his brow and pulled his hair over his ears. By the look a that fizzog yow ay got anythin wuff pawnin, he remembered this pawner saying. Could that be why he was being cheated. Did the pawners see him coming. Was anything fair. Was He really there.

His fears were released upon entry when he spotted the woman tending to the cabinets.

Simmy ay in? he said.

The woman gasped and spun around clutching her hand to her chest. Frit me to death! Day hear ya come in.

Michael smiled and apologised. Then a brief pause. It seemed as though the woman needed time to catch her breath.

No, Simmy's under the weather today. Juss me om afraid, but I can help ya with anything. Iss the job of a metalsmith to know about this sort a thing!

Yowm a metalsmith?

Think it was juss Simmy? She held a hand out to Michael. Name's Mary.

Michael shook and introduced himself. Her hands were delicate and warm, not what you might expect from a metalsmith. She smiled and her cheeks lifted and obscured her shining eyes. He felt something from her, something he had forgot possible since before the birth of Luke. It was as though she knew all his troubles and only wanted to help. Surely this woman with all her warmth would provide him with good news. Surely she woe cheat him.

So what have ya brought for us? Or is it a new something ya fancy buying?

Selling somethin.

Well what have ya got? Want to bring it over to the desk?

Michael fetched the bundle and passed it across to Mary. She looked at it and then back up at him and smiled. Surprise, is it? she said.

Iss gold.

Gold? she said, unwrapping the parcel.

Ar.

Well, yowm in luck, gold prices am quite high at the moment. Sure we can make ya—

A pause. Michael felt his heart jump. Mary's face went from bright to dim as her words were snuffed out by what her eyes beheld. The smile that held her cheeks high and obscured her eyes fell and a frown formed. As much as he day want to believe it, he already knew the words that were to follow. Still, she looked through the bundle with concern.

Ah, Mary said after a moment. Om afraid this ay gold.

What? Not ye as well. What is it with all a ye.

Me as well? Have ya taken this to some other shop?

Thass gold, Michael said firmly.

Love, om sorry to let ya down but this ay proper gold. Where did ya get it?

Michael stared at her. Her voice was soft and welcoming, her head tilted slightly in a consoling manner, like he was a lost child she had come upon in the middle of a fete. What she presented with her demeanour and what came from her mouth set him with conflicting emotions. Could she too be cheating him? After all, why could she not have seen him coming like the rest.

He snatched the gold and stepped away.

Michael, she said.

Ye doe know me.

Om sorry iss not the news ya was clearly after, love, but weem a business, an that juss ay—

Yowm worse than the others, Michael said venomously. Mary drew back and closed her mouth as though she were the wick of a candle being snuffed out.

As soon as he left the shop it finally sunk in. He could try the jeweller just outside the village. Even though he could already see the jeweller's face and hear his words, he went anyway.

It was getting late. The light of day was failing and shops were closing. Michael knew the way to the jeweller but day know if he would arrive in time for closing. Even though his hope was all but gone, he ran. He ran past the sparse string of houses and shops that vied for space in the village, past osses and carts and around trees and across the common. He cut through Norton Road and followed the Ryders Hayes trail until he lost sight of his feet and whatever was five feet in front of – an ow could she cheat ye juss like the rest a them but watch ya step the cut is cold an ye doe want to fall cheatin ye theym all at it all as bad as each other all sin ye comin telegraphed ya position in life an ye think they being common people an all would see ya plight an help ye out but maybe iss juss ye own fault not seein the gold for what it really is what yowve wasted so much time an health an fitness on so why now ye risk it why goo runnin but ye cor let it goo thass why why let it goo now without findin out truly from a good honest person but then if the answer ay to ya likin ow can ye – then he noticed the trail open up where lamppostlight beckoned like bonfires of commerce and trade. He breathed harshly the bitingly cold air that sent coughing fits up and out his gullet. Against a lamppost he gathered his breath and spat black phlegm into the dirt before walking on to the jewellers.

The lights in the shop were out. The jeweller was in the middle of fetching small plywood boxes and placing them onto a cart.

Still open? Michael said.

Closed for the day om afraid, the jeweller said.

Om sorry, Michael said. I juss ran over here to catch ye before closing. I just want some metal valuing, thass all.

The jeweller stopped loading his cart and looked him up and down, still muddied and black with soot and soil. Tell ye what, he said, help me load the rest a these and oll have a quick butcher's.

Michael nodded and lifted the remaining boxes swiftly. They were large but light, or they felt light. This jeweller seemed kind. Perchance the others were indeed driving the price of his treasure down to make a profit on his lack of knowledge in metals. Perchance this jeweller who was willing to show this slight bit of kindness would be fair.

Inside they lit a large gas lamp and illuminated the bundle of sparkling metal and rock.

Ah, the jeweller said almost instantly, this is interesting.

Whass it wuff?

Not much. Call this fool's gold. It can be med into something pretty alright, but not much value in it. Especially in this state.

Michael sighed and ran the back of his hand against his forehead that sent streams of sweat down his forearm. Yowm bein honest?

Of course. Why wouldn't I be?

What would ye give for it now then?

The jeweller sniffed and opened a drawer behind him and fetched out some coins. He held a thrupenny bit into the light. Thass for rough, he said. Can do ye a receipt for ten percent on what I make on it in jewellery an all if you like.

Michael looked down at the coin. Blackened and crude. The crown stamped high at the top of the tails of it. He picked it up and turned it over. Victoria in perfect side profile.

He thought back to Smithy, the pawner in Dudley, and how Cain had been angry with his valuation. Had he too offered a thrupenny, or nothing at all?

Michael nodded and nodded, more angrily as the seconds went on. He felt a fist of hot ash rise up his throat and tried with all his pride to stop it from growing. It day work. His eyes welled. He clenched his teeth and watched the coin smudge and blur before it turned into a wet image of plain light.

Night fell over the village. A blizzard emptied from the sky. It whipped sideways across his face. The redness that usually mossed the horizons replaced by endless mountains of white.

The baker recognised him and said, Ow bist.

Michael asked for a loaf and handed him the thrupenny bit. He was returned a few feeble coins change. He slid them into the toe of his pocket and waited.

There was a woman with her young girl in the shop. The girl buzzing around him like a dragonfly. He looked down at her and smiled. She showed him her teeth.

The woman held out her hand and said, Liza, come. The girl glided to her mother. He looked up at her and smiled again. She looked away.

The baker passed over the bread. He thanked him and stopped at the door. Looked at the woman. Leant in towards her. Gritted his teeth and said venomously, Ye really am a piece a rubbish, ay ya.

Michael outside the school in the white quiet. The flakes fell slow and calm now. His jaw stiff by clenched teeth not brought on by the cold but as the easiest way to ward off tears. He had spoken to more people today than he wanted to. He kept reliving his conversations with them in his head. It was that woman in the bakery that he saw and heard repeat in his mind's eye the most though. He prided himself on being a good person, and he let the broiling hot magma that sat in the back of his throat loose upon her. Even now, after everything that had happened, he felt regret for that. He hated that he did and he day know why.

Behind the yellow windows people moved about. All of them dark shapes behind the misted panes. A few parents waited. The main door opened. Kids spilled out like water pumped from a pit. No Luke. Some of the kids went off walking on with each other, others met their parents. Michael stood clutching the hardened bread underarm. Luke emerged last. He was with a man who wrapped a scarf around his neck before stepping out.

Michael approached them. Son, he said.

Father!

Michael drew his arm around the boy and brought him close. Missed ye, he said. And he had. He felt a warmth come from the lad, a homeliness.

What ya doin ere?

Come to pick yarrup, obviously.

The man behind Luke held a surprised face. Oh, hello. Om Mr Richardson. He held his hand out and shook Michael's. I was juss about to walk him back. We live not far apart now.

Thank ye. Ow's he gettin on?

Good. Better. Seems to be gettin used to it, this learnin business. The teacher winked at Luke and clucked his tongue. Well, I bess leave ya to it.

Good evenin.

Nice to meet ya.

The teacher walked up the road and they followed shortly after. He held the bread under one wing and the boy under the other.

So, school gerrin better?

I suppose.

I know yowd prefer not to goo. But iss for the bess. Ye doe wanna end up like me do ye? Workin in the pits.

Yow always say that, but whass so wrung wi workin in the pits?

All sorts. Black in ya lungs. Yowve sin me. Really bad I was after that triple shift. Teks it out a ye. An yowm down there wi loads of other blokes. Sweaty. Some a them naked.

Naked?

Ar.

Luke scrunched his face up. But iss cold, he said.

Not down there. Iss boilin down the pits. Worse than workin in the blazin sun an all because a the soot from the coal, an the gases, an the pitfloor sometimes floods an as to be pumped out wi a engine. Thass when the roof doe come down on ye an all.

Their feet crunched on the snow. Luke was silent for a moment. Then he said, Oll try me bess at school, Father.

He looked down to the boy beside him. His head held up huge shining eyes, fireblue like burning copper. There was still a glimpse. He could be different. Straight-backed, clever, strong. There had to be another way. And he had to stay alive to see it through.

Michael tousled Luke's hair with his blackened paw and bent down and raked in bundles of snow. Come on, he said, get ye some ammunition.

Luke started for the wall aside him and started to scrape snow. Michael threw his ball and it powdered against the boy's back and he shouted before turning around in almost manic excitement and returned fire. Michael tried to run away but slipped on the track and bowled over. Luke clumped more snow hastily into rough shapes and peppered his father. They both laughed as the boy helped the man to his feet.

XXIII

FATHER and son outside the door. They stamped the snow from their shoes before entering. Inside they were hit by a wall of soft delicious heat. That nice kind of heat only felt in winter.

He dropped the bread on the sidetable. Jane was coming through the back door with a small bucket of firewood. So thass where yowve bin, she said, dropping the bucket and blowing upward, sending her fringe flailing. Thought Mr Richardson was walkin yow back.

Me too, but Father's back. Told ya he would be.

Luke, goo to ya room an let me have a word wi ya father for a minute.

Why?

Juss goo. Oll call ya when tea's done.

He looked at his father, who nodded and said, Goo on, son.

At the fireside Michael groaned as he slowly lowered himself into the chair. He felt every muscle and bone shudder. Looked up. She watched him.

Well?

He day want to tell her, or even speak at all. After a pause he gave in to the easiest form of telling he could think of. Iss wuffless, he said.

What?

Ye gone deaf now?

What. How can it be?

He shook his head, faced her and spat venom. Tay gold. Ast three different people.

She raised a hand to her head and wiped the sweat from it and stared at the floor. Her eyes were darting as though she was following a scuttling mouse.

Well, what is it then?

Does it matter.

What did yow get for it?

He motioned his head backwards to the bread. Her eyes met it. She let her weight go against the dinner table and sighed.

The tick of the clock. The spit of the fire. After a moment she said, Well, we doe need it anyway.

He stared into the flames with empty eyes.

Do we? Jane reiterated.

Doe get it, do ye.

Whass that supposed to mean?

I thought. I really thought I wor gooin to find it. So I was coming back. An then there it was. Fount again. Everythin I did was justified in that bundle. Really felt like He was guidin me. Felt like the land was finally givin back. What for?

A silence.

Yowm here, she said, thass what matters. Om earnin for his school now. We cor wait about for gods.

Michael shook his head and ran his hand through his hair. Matted with soot and sweat. He wanted to say it wor just getting by, it had become more than that. He day want to see her work. Day want to see her caged as he was. But he had lost.

The false gold plagued his mind. Everything that had happened because of it. That same question kept coming to him: What for?

Should a took that money off Lawrence, he said.

What?

Another silence.

After a while, she shouted the boy. Time for tea. Potato and leek soup again.

◆

They ate their meal quietly save for Luke going on and on about something to do with school or asking his father what he had been doing. Michael gave short answers. He always tried to put on a brave face for the boy, to make sure he was savouring his company, making him happy. He hated for the boy to know the truth of his feelings. But since they had got back home, he had become far too tired. The heat was wrapping him up and the thin soup was knocking him out.

And Cain was out there alone in all that cold and all that dark. And Michael and his family in the house that not less than two days ago Cain was sitting in, all changed by luck and divine intervention and for what. It seemed like they were better off with this place. He was starting to think they wor. Nobody was.

He left his meal unfinished and washed up in the outhouse and said goodnight to Luke and went to bed. He day pay much attention to the new room, the coolness of it, or the bed or anything around it. He simply sank into the straw mattress and pulled the blankets to his chin and closed his eyes.

Michael was woken by the dull light of the morning through the curtainless window. He'd had a dreamful sleep but could not remember the dream, only that he did have one and now it was out of reach. Lost like the breath of a bull in winter.

He sat up in the bed and felt the cold wood against his feet. He tried to get up and groaned with pain. He slowly stretched to relax his muscles. His feet pattered towards the door. He looked down at the bed and amongst the foliage of quilts and covers a pair of wideawake eyes stared at him.

Mornin, he said.

Still they stared, dark and quiet like stagnant wells.

In the front room, the clock on the fireplace said it was twenty to seven. November twelfth. He tended to the dotted embers amongst the grey coals of last night's fire. Added more paper and wood and coal and watched the hands of flames wave upwards.

Took the brass poker and fixed himself some toasted bread on the fire. It tasted like old wood. The day got brighter as the fire crackled in the quiet. What he woe a gave for a nice piece of roasted bass or roach. He washed down the bread with water from the communal well. What he woe a gave for ale or wine. Wine was always something he'd wanted to try. At least once.

He noticed again the red chest in the corner. It looked different in the morning's glow. Whether out of tiredness or something else he became transfixed by it and sat watching it until past seven. Then he got up and opened it. Why did he halfexpect something inside? He closed and lifted it up under his arm. Behind the lodging was the well. Michael stepped barefooted over the snow until he reached the stone top. He placed the chest at its roots and pushed off the wooden lid. Across the surface of the water was a shine from the white snowclouds, stamped by a black mass. It wor until he fetched up the chest and leant back over the well that he realised the mass was himself. A true reflection. He held the chest over and let it go. The thump was followed by waves that sent his reflection spiralling around the surface. He watched it for a moment before traipsing back inside.

XXIV

If ye want somethin, tek it, he remembered Cain saying. And in his mind he cor agree with it but sometimes he did things without thinking, almost as if his body was not his own. The same such driving force that felt to him as though it came deep from the belly of the earth, sent him out to work early to do the only thing he knew. What else was there? When ye wake, ye work.

The violet morning light was creeping over the veiled horizon and he heard what sounded not like the crow of a cockerel but hens arguing, perhaps over an egg. He noticed the neighbour was also leaving early.

Mornin, Michael said.

I remember yow, the neighbour said. John. He held out his hand.

Michael. They shook hands.

Out early, ay ya?

Ar. Missed yesterdy so thought od get down there earlier today.

Ay sure it works like that, John said.

Where ye off then?

John pointed over the bungalows towards the creek. Catchin frogs, he said. Should still be about now.

What for?

Goo well in stews, obviously.

Michael raised his eyebrows and said, Am things that bad?

Life's life, ayit, John said. Bess give in to it afore it swallows ye. John went past and took crunching sounds with him under his boots.

His walk to the pits was longer now. He crossed the cornfields. A wide white blanket. His boots spoiled the perfect path of snow. Soon these fields of white would be melted away and broken in for the spring harvest. He decided to try and enjoy these winter walks whilst they lasted. The land changes faster than stays the same.

He looked at the past few days with wellrested eyes. He again had to swallow his pride. He had been ready to when he first gave up on the gold, it should be simpler the second time. Why was it more difficult? He was teased and taunted by the land, by the Lord.

Michael went over a stile and through a brush of naked trees. Brown rotting leaves upturned in the grey light. At the frozen creek a little egret camouflaged against the snowy reposed bank. Only its thin black legs and beak stood out.

Why ye fishin on a frozen lake? he shouted.

The little egret was still. Beak creekwards. And how thin it was. Pencil-like. Impossible to break through the thick sheet of ice built up overnight.

After watching it for a moment, tears stood in his eyes.

The sky was moving over the iron bridge. Ashenwhite like spent coal through the fire grate. Under the bridge a pair of workosses struggled to stay on the bank of the cut. Michael pressed himself into the hedgerow. Along the cut a crunching. An icebreaker narrowboat. It had a thick wooden protrusion that held firm in the centre of the boat that looked something like a battering ram. Men stood at the front of the barge and rocked it from side to side, leaning over the nose and inspecting the ice. It cracked and split in veins lengthways along the surface. As the osses passed, he fell deeper into the hedge and felt himself sticking to the branches.

The barge left behind islands of ice that bobbed on the rippling black water. Canada geese followed, nipping their beaks amongst the freshly exposed undergrowth. On the bridge and along the bank came onlookers, chatting and smoking.

He squirmed out of the hedge and instantly they were upon him. Brushing past him. Wading through him. They spoke nonsense and laughed whilst marvelling at the icebreaker barge.

Michael on the bank of the colliery already black with footfall. It was bordered by murky grey sludge. The white sky scaffolded with slow black ropes escaping the chimney.

The bankswomen and men pushing waggons and buckets and driving osses and standing atop the pits. The wheel moving as it did yesterday and the day before and through each night and each day. The land may change, but these things of men stay the same.

He approached the pit top. A few bankswomen were stood waiting for the next call from below. The cage was idle. He had almost forgotten what it looked like. Cold rusted iron with wide trellises. The bankswomen watched him step into the cage. Nightshift still down there, one said.

Not in my stall, he said.

How ya know?

Juss send it, Abigail.

The man's too early.

Who cares anyroad?

Let the undermanager sort it.

Listen to ya mates, he said.

The cage started to lower. The frostbitten chains sounded fit to snap. He left everything above.

By the time the cage hit the floor there were night-workers waiting to load their tubs onto the cage. They frowned up at him in the lamplight. He ignored them and went past. The usual undermanager wor there. It was a small bald man that sat upon a stool at the top of the inbye rolling cigarettes under the Davy. He paid Michael no attention when he fetched a pickaxe from the toolbin and waded through the pitfloor.

After picking for almost two hours, the morning shift came down. He pissed against the wall and rested his arms before raking and shovelling his pickings into the tub. Mostly slack. He looked at the coalface. Black glistens lamptinted in the dark. He wor sure why he hoped for anything different. It was impossible, he knew that now, yet still he looked for golden shine, like the little egret looking for fish at the creek.

Hullo?

Michael turned to the voice that came highpitched like that of a young lad or grown lass. A figure was stood in the stall opening, as tall as he but far slenderer.

What, Michael said.

Of bin sent to this stall.

Michael took up the Davy lamp and held it towards the figure, lighting him up in orange and yellow flicker. Ow old bin ye, chap, he said.

Eighteen, sir.

He nodded and held out his hand. Michael.

Om James.

Bess get to werk then.

Yes sir.

They hit the wall with their axes. It felt like a lifetime ago when he was the new one to this mine. He cor help but see himself in the young man.

Fust job, Michael said.

Second.

It seemed James day have a fancy for talk just as much as he.

Midshift. Michael swung the pick underarm, beating the lower wall where a thin yet deep cavern was forming an overhanging ledge of rock. The slow cackling of chains.

He turned and saw in the dimness a child attaching himself to Michael's stallcart. Nay, he shouted. Nay.

The child's silhouette stopped still.

Michael was unable to tell whether the lad was looking at him or not. Leave it, he said.

A pause. The unlatching of chains. Down the track a shuffle.

Thass his job, James said.

Not on this stall it ay. We tek our own tubs.

James sighed. Why mek the job harder on yaself? He's gerrin paid.

Shouldn't be down here when theym that young.

It ay all bad. I worked that job for years.

Michael stopped and stretched out his back and grimaced. Ye did?

Ar. Now look at me. Fit as.

Michael nodded. Ar, now look at ye. Still here.

I ay the any one, James said, returning his pick to the wall.

The mine was quieter than usual. Michael noticed in the neighbouring stalls those men who had offered him a drink a few days ago. One of them looked at him and nodded. Day see ye comin in, he said.

Got in early, Michael said, pushing his cart along the tunnel. He felt even in the darkness of the tunnel the miners burning holes of their own through him as he moved along the track.

He sent the cart up the cage but day wait for it to come back down. He waded the sump and back through the tunnel. He moved with habit now. The mine an extension of him and he of it.

All the morning through he had thought about Jane and Luke. He remembered what she said about waiting for gods. He had to forget his pride and move on, but day want to think about it all any more. So, he picked. He picked and picked, for what else could he do. He picked until he stopped thinking about other things. It was he and the earth and them only. He picked until blisters burst on the webs of skin between his fingers, until stinging hot sweat swarmed his eyes, until hit after hit a trickle of water escaped through the coalface.

He set the pickaxe at his feet. Reached out and fingered the shimmering liquid. It was dark and thin and hot. It pulsed from the wall as if it was bleeding. It looked like Cain's leg. When it reached the low ledge of rock it dripped into the earth like some tiny waterfall. He craned his neck and shouted the other men. They came and saw the waterfall and reached with their hands each of them and felt its warm lick. It wor a problem as it was, they said. Bess to leave it til it dries out though, said one.

James knelt and observed it with a lamp. Fuck sake, he said, fust fuckin shift. Then he took off down the tunnel. Gooin topside for a smoke, he snapped.

Someone's a bit of a blouse ay they? said one of the miners as they returned to their stalls laughing. Michael was straightfaced, watching the coalface.

He had sat on the far side of the stall against some timber for a while. Was this the last cruel take? Forcing him to watch as the little waterfall dried out? It could take all day. The mine had always been boggy anyroad. A bit more water woe hurt.

He rose and took up the axe and went to the far side of the stall and carried on working. He was breaking off huge chunks of pure sharp black coal. Nonslack. He hit the wall with everything he had left in him. Hit after hit after hit after hit after hit after hit his arms tightened and his muscles were set ablaze on the inside, this mine that brought life yet death, pleasure yet pain. He pulled more and more heaps of coal off the wall and sent them thudding onto his boots and crashing about him like a torrent. It wor until he felt the cold slosh of water wave against his ankles that he noticed the leak had grown to a thick stream.

Shit, Michael said. He dropped his axe and stumbled across his stall and fell onto his knees and stared into the stream. There he saw everything laid out before him. His past, present and future. His father, his son, Jane, Cain, himself and everyone else he ever knew, all amongst the decaying insides of the earth. It was Mercia. Redblooded and full of rage. It was then that it all became clear to him. Everything he had done before had brought him here, like it had done to everyone that was and would do to everyone that is.

The smacks of axe against wall were drowned out by a deep gurgling growl as the coalface started to cave. His heart leapt in his chest. His legs were frozen. He turned away to shout warning but instead the cold surge forced only a sharp pneumatic hiss of breath as it reached out and gathered him in its enormous arms. Above along the bank a wind forced all snow and frost to be gone, where at

ACKNOWLEDGEMENTS

The author wishes to thank the Booker Prize Foundation and the University of East Anglia. Without their funding he would not have been able to create this novel. He would also like to thank all who helped during the editing process, including Rex Rowley, Omer Tennenhaus, Jay Wai, Patrick Ball, Andrew Evans and Philip Langeskov. The author is most grateful to Kim Wiles, Paris Sinclair and all his family for their support.

This is a novel inspired by real events and informed by extensive historical research. The Walsall Local History Archives were an indispensable source of relevant information, accounts and maps.

Lastly, the author would like to dedicate this work to those that died in the Pelsall Hall Colliery disaster of 1872:

Thomas Starkey, married.
Thomas Starkey, grandson of the above.
John Starkey, married, one child.
Michael Cash, married.
Charles Cash, unmarried son of above.
Thomas Hollis, married, three children.
Joseph Hollis, married, two children.
John Hayward, married, seven children.
Charles Capewell, widower.
Edward Williams, married.
Richard Hyde, married, four children.
Charles Astbury, married, two children.
George Ball, married, one child.
William Richards, married.
John Quarters, married.
John Hubbard.
Frank Dukes.
Thomas Orcas.
Stephen Lawton, a boy.
John Roberts, a boy.
Thomas Coleman, a boy.